for the

Love

of the

Lady

The Noble Hearts, Book 4

CALLIE HUTTON

Author's website: http://calliehutton.com/
Cover design by Erin Dameron-Hill
Manufactured in the United States of America

First Print Edition September 2018

ISBN 10: 1727340868
ISBN 13: 978-1727340860

ABOUT THE BOOK

Lord Henry Pomeroy's three daughters are finally married and happily settled in their own homes. He's looking forward to grandbabies and the company of Lady Crampton, the woman who acted as chaperone and companion to his daughters these past four years—and stole his heart in the meantime. Except she is moving out of his house!

Lady Selina Crampton has fallen hopelessly in love with her employer. Now that his youngest daughter is married, there is no longer a reason for her to remain since her work has come to an end. Marriage is not possible, and the time has come to confront her demons and tell him why she has refused his numerous offers of marriage.

It appears everyone is going to have their happy ending...except Lady Selina and Lord Henry.

Thank you for choosing to read *For the Love of the Lady*.

I love my fans, and as a special treat,

I have something extra for you at the end of the story.

Enjoy!

DEDICATION

To Maria Connor, the best personal assistant ever.

PROLOGUE

July, 1822
London, England

Lord Henry Pomeroy settled into the most comfortable chair in his library, a glass of brandy in one hand, the latest book he'd been reading in the other. With all the nonsense surrounding his youngest daughter Marigold's wedding, he'd had little time to relax with his favorite things to do. Read and drink a brandy.

The only thing missing was Selina, Lady Crampton, the woman who acted as chaperone and companion to his two younger daughters before they married. Generally, she joined him in the evenings when she wasn't accompanying Marigold to an event. She would sit and work on her embroidery while he read her various interesting passages from his latest book.

Where was the blasted woman, anyway? The bride and groom had departed two hours ago, and his other two daughters had arrived from preparing their sister for her wedding night at her new husband's home, collected their husbands, and left. It had been a long day, and he was more than happy to have it done with.

He shifted in his chair, waiting for her arrival. Finally, the door opened and she entered. He immediately relaxed. "You know I can't concentrate on my book with you not here." He smiled at her and handed her a glass of sherry as was their practice.

She settled on her seat, took a tiny sip of sherry, and placed the glass on a small table in front of them. She laid her hands on her lap. Taking a deep breath, she said, "Henry, we must talk."

Sensing something disturbed her, he lowered his book and gave her his full attention. He'd found over the years that when it came to women, lovely as they were, the sentence "We need to talk" usually preceded tears and recriminations. "What is it, my dear?"

She raised her chin and stared him directly in his eyes. "Henry, I am presenting my resignation." She took out a sheet of vellum from her gown pocket and held it out toward him.

Henry studied her carefully and set his glass down. "What are you talking about?"

"My resignation, Henry. I am resigning my

position. I must leave."

"Selina, it has been a difficult couple of weeks. We are both tired. I don't wish to play games. Of course, you cannot resign."

She stood and paced. "Of course, I cannot *not* resign."

Finally realizing she was serious, he tamped down his anxiety and stood and placed his hands on her shoulders. "What is the matter, Selina?"

She burst into tears, and he wrapped his arms around her and laid her cheek against him. She sobbed on his chest for a bit, then he handed her a handkerchief. She looked up at him with a red nose, swollen eyes, and took a deep, shuddering breath. "My work here is finished."

"I can see you are very upset, so I won't make light of your concerns, but you cannot leave."

"I was hired as a chaperone and companion to your daughters." She sniffed and waved her hand around. "Not that I've done such a wonderful job since they were all in a family way when they married."

Henry leaned back. "Marigold, too?"

"Yes," she nodded. "You see, I wasn't even *good* at the job."

He pushed back the hair that had fallen from her tidy arrangement of curls onto her shoulder. "You have done the most remarkable job ever."

She huffed. "How is that, Henry?"

"You run my home, you deal with the staff.

You keep me company in the evenings. More importantly, you've made me realize my life could continue after my dear departed wife left us." He made the sign of the cross. He took her hands and kissed each knuckle. "You taught me to believe in love again, Selina. And—"

She tightened her lips and closed her eyes. "Don't say it, Henry."

He cupped her face, stroking her soft cheeks with his thumbs. "I will say it. Over and over again until you agree. Marry me, my love."

With tear-filled eyes, she slowly shook her head. "No. I've told you before, Henry. I cannot marry you."

CHAPTER ONE

Lord Pomeroy looked up from his newspaper as Lady Crampton entered the breakfast room. Her eyes were puffy, and she looked as though she hadn't slept a wink all night. Neither had he. After her announcement that she was packing up and leaving his home, and still refused to marry him, he paced in his room and fought the urge to go to her bedchamber and demand answers until he'd nearly worn out the carpet and the sun peeked over the horizon.

Ordinarily, they would spend the night together, but since he did not wish to continue the argument, he'd stayed away from her. With the mood she'd been in when she made her announcement, he felt it was best to leave her be for the night. Not something he was happy about. "Good morning, my dear."

Selina offered him a sad smile. "Good morning."

He remained silent while she filled her plate with the usual breakfast offerings: one boiled egg, one piece of toast, and an orange. She sat at her place, and the footman poured her tea. Henry watched as she fixed her tea and tapped the egg shell with her spoon.

He could stand it no longer. "Selina, we must speak about this dilemma."

Her hand paused as she held the tea cup close to her lips. "There is no dilemma, Henry. I will visit with Lady Penrose today to learn if the girls and I may have our rooms back."

"I don't want you to leave."

"I have no choice. I don't want to leave. You must know that. But don't you see how improper it would be for me to stay? I have two young daughters who will be thrust into the complex world of the *ton* in less than a year. They will not be welcomed with open arms into Society if their mother is considered a whore."

Henry sucked in a breath, his blood pumping so hard through his heart, he thought it would explode. "Never say that. Never, Selina. You are not a whore, and you are not to even think such a thing."

She turned her head away from him, her adorable stubborn chin raised. "I have no place here anymore."

"I shall hire you as my housekeeper." He felt quite smug.

Selina regarded him with raised brows. "You have a housekeeper."

"I shall fire her."

"What? Don't be ridiculous, Henry. Mrs.

Woolford has been with you for years."

"Yes. You're right. I cannot fire her." He took a sip of coffee. "Then I shall have two housekeepers." He studied her. "Can you cook?"

"Yes, I can cook, and no, I won't allow you to fire your cook, either."

"Then you must marry me."

Selina placed her hands in her lap and studied him. "Henry, I cannot marry you. I am sorry. I love you, I know you love me, but it is not possible. At least not right now, anyway."

He pounced on her mumbled last words. "What was that you said?"

She shook her head. "Nothing."

Henry shoved his chair back and stood, leaning his hands on the table, bringing his face close to Selina's. He could see the surprise in her eyes and the slight flush on her cheeks. She apparently had not wanted him to hear what she said, but he was not letting it go. "You said something about 'not right away.' What did you mean by that?"

She sighed deeply and shook her head. "You will not cease to continue asking me, will you?"

"Marrying you? No, not at all. As you said, I love you and you love me. However, you won't marry me. I feel I have the right to insist on knowing why."

"Lord Crampton."

He eased back into his seat. "What about Lord Crampton? He is dead."

"Yes."

"Do you mean the new Lord Crampton?"

She shook her head.

After allowing her a few moments of silence, he prodded. "So, what about Lord Crampton?"

"He was a … difficult man."

Henry stiffened in his chair. "Did he hurt you? I shall dig him up and kill him again."

"No, no. Nothing like that. At least not physically, anyway." She began to fiddle with her spoon, not meeting his eyes.

Henry had known Lord Crampton from their time in Parliament together. The man had been older than Selina by almost three decades. Henry had always assumed her deceased husband had been anxious for an heir, which was why he married a young bride. She could not have been more than eighteen when she wed Crampton who was then at least in his early fifties.

He remembered Crampton as being a windbag, very impressed with his own consequence. He'd sported a full-faced beard, a rather rotund body, and a balding head.

Certainly not someone to whom a young girl would be attracted.

"He was quite possessive. I always had the feeling he didn't trust me—or rather other men."

"He kept a close watch on you?"

"Yes. We would return from a ball, and I would receive a tirade all the way home on the gentlemen who had paid attention to me. In some cases, he even had a list." She huffed with righteous indignation. "For heaven's sake, I was a married woman and not one to encourage other men's attentions."

"What has all this to do with not marrying me? Are you afraid all husbands are the same? Do you not trust me to treat you well?"

She laid her hand on his resting on the table. "Of course not, Henry. I know you very well and am sure you would never treat me so."

"Then what is it, my love? Why refuse to consider both of our happiness?" He fought the panic rising in his chest. He could not watch her walk out of his life. They were friends, lovers, and he needed her like he needed his next breath of air.

"As I said, Lord Crampton was not a very nice person. For the most part, he ignored our daughters, being angered from their birth that they were girls. But I know in his own strange way he loved them. And that is why I cannot marry you."

Henry stared at her for a full minute as she stared back at him. He licked his dry lips. "That doesn't make sense."

"Lord Crampton was quite wealthy."

Although he believed her, he'd always wondered what had happened to the man's wealth once he died. It was a subject Selina had never spoken about, and he was reluctant to ask, since the need to support herself and her daughters had brought her into his life.

All of Crampton's entailed property, of course, along with the income from those properties went to his heir, the man's third cousin, but there should have been money enough to provide for Selina and his daughters upon his death. If nothing else, whoever drew up the settlement papers when they first married would have made sure there was a widow's portion set aside for Selina in the event of Crampton's death. "Can you explain further what you mean, my dear?"

"His lordship managed, I was never sure how, to move the money my father negotiated for me during the marriage settlements into an account he had use of. That money was spent. Therefore, when he died, I had nothing."

"What about his estate, his will?"

Her words followed a deep sigh. "He set his will up in such a way that I receive no money and all the funds go to the girls to provide for their Seasons and dowries."

"And…" Somehow, he knew this was not going to be good.

"They will only receive the money if I do not remarry. Otherwise, it all goes to his third cousin, his heir and the man who he despised most of his life."

Selina watched the confusion in Henry's eyes turn

to anger. "He did *what?*"

"That's what his solicitor advised me after the funeral. It was confirmed when we had the reading of the will. I have nothing, and the girls have nothing until they reach their come-out age. Then they can have all the money they want, providing it goes for gowns, slippers, ribbons— all the things young ladies need when they enter the marriage mart—with the balance of the funds to be split between them once the second one marries."

"Did the solicitor give any reason why Crampton elected to distribute his estate in such a manner?"

She gave him a half smile. "Yes. It was written into the will. He said the reason he left me nothing was because I had not produced a male heir, so I had not 'earned' a settlement."

Henry let out with quite a colorful curse and ran his fingers through his hair. "Why have you not told me before now? Furthermore, that doesn't sound legal to me. Did you contest his will?"

"With what, Henry? I had no money to hire a solicitor, and his lordship's solicitor told me he couldn't help me because it would be a conflict of interest."

"No doubt *his* interest."

"No, Mr. Darwin is an honorable man. And the reason I hadn't told you before now is because I was humiliated at how my husband had treated me. Since there was no reason for us to marry—"

"—until now."

"I kept the information to myself."

Henry stood and pulled her to her feet. "We will fight this together. I won't allow a dead man to dictate whom I shall and shall not marry."

She laid her head against his chest, the solid sound of his heartbeats soothing her. Maybe she could not marry him until both girls were married and their dowries paid, but she could certainly enjoy his love and companionship until then.

But she could no longer remain in his house. She lifted her head. "So you see, I cannot continue on here. The fact that I spent even one night here after Marigold's marriage will leave me open to gossip."

"I don't care about gossip. I care about you." He lowered his head and kissed her softly, but the contact soon turned into something strong and passionate. "Stay one more night," he murmured against her lips.

She pushed on his chest. "No. I cannot. If I don't leave now, it will only grow harder. If I want Phoebe and Prudence to have successful come-outs and make decent matches, there can be no shadow cast over my reputation."

"Of course, you are aware of the number of women who enjoy a lover's attentions while their husbands visit their mistresses, and their daughters do quite well with suitable matches."

"Yes, but they don't blatantly live with those lovers. Everything with the *ton* is appearances, as you well know."

Henry sighed and dropped his arms. "I am afraid you are right, my dear."

She smoothed the wrinkles from her gown. "May I have the carriage to travel to Lady Penrose?"

"Absolutely. You may have anything you want." He winked at her. "Including me."

***

Thankfully, Selina had kept in touch with Lady Penrose, enjoying her company at various social events and visiting for tea. She was a lovely woman, a widow also, with a huge house. Her husband's title had passed onto his eldest son from an earlier marriage, but Penrose had been kind enough to leave her the unentailed charming home in Mayfair where she resided.

With no children of her own, she had been more than happy to take Selina and the girls in after Crampton's death. She had been appalled at what Crampton had done and insisted on Selina writing to every relative, no matter how remote, both in her family and Crampton's family, to seek assistance.

Since she and Crampton had been only children, there were no siblings to help, and because his heir had hated Crampton as much as he'd hated him back, she'd shied away from asking for any help from him. Hopefully, her influence on the twins would counter any nastiness they may have inherited from their father and his family.

It was a beautiful summer day as she traversed the distance from Pomeroy House to Lady Penrose's townhouse. Bright green leaves on the trees quivered softly with the slight wind, and the scent of flowers filled the air from various gardens along the roadway. Despite being only a short distance from Pomeroy House, with the traffic, it took her nearly a half hour to arrive.

She'd written a note to Lady Penrose the prior afternoon when she realized Marigold's marriage meant she would be displaced. It should have occurred to her during the wedding preparations, but she'd been so swept up in the romance of Marigold and Jonathan that she'd overlooked that minor fact. If she stayed with the man she loved, she would disgrace her daughters and ruin their chances for an acceptable match.

She would have to dip into her savings to compensate Lady Penrose for her kindness in allowing them to stay. Henry had tried to insist on paying Lady Penrose, but she could not allow that. For heaven's sake, that would make her a kept woman!

So many times she had struggled with the thought that she had barely enough money to purchase even an ice at Gunters, but very soon she could walk into any exclusive modiste shop with Prudence and Phoebe and order up as many gowns for their come-out as she liked. Working as Marigold and Juliet's chaperone and companion had at least given her the freedom to spend a bit of money on herself.

She'd tucked away almost a hundred pounds in the past four years, so hopefully she would not have to seek employment any time soon. If she were careful with her coins, she might be able to forestall having to take a position until after the girls' come-out.

Unless Henry waited for her to become free, then she would not need employment. She blinked away the tears at the thought of him taking up with another woman. One who was free to marry him.

The carriage came to a rolling stop in front of the tidy townhouse with the teal blue door. The colorful summer flowers in front of Lady Penrose's townhouse were in full bloom as she climbed from the carriage and made her way up the steps.

She drew in a quick breath when the front door opened, and a man stepped out. For the first time in four years she came face-to-face with the new Lord Crampton. She had rarely seen him because rumor was he spent a great deal of time in Greece, where he had been living when he came into her deceased husband's title.

Once or twice over the years, they had been at the same events, but he had never approached her, nor she him. Their last interaction had been at the reading of Lord Crampton's will when the new Viscount had stormed out of the library after discovering he'd inherited the title, but the fortune was tied up for the girls' Season and dowries.

He bowed and tipped his hat. "Good morning, my lady. How nice to see you." He looked around and smiled, then took her hand in his. "A lovely day, is it not?" Before she could stop him, he kissed the back of her glove and continued down the steps swinging his cane.

What the devil is he doing here?

CHAPTER TWO

Henry walked to the window in his study as he awaited the arrival of his solicitor, Mr. Barnes. The sound of Selina running up and down the stairs as she packed for the move to Mrs. Penrose's home gave him a sense of urgency to get the matter straightened out as quickly as possible.

His thoughts drifted back to when Selina had first appeared in his life four years prior. It had been a lovely day such as the present one when his butler stepped into the library and held out his hand. "You have a visitor, my lord. She awaits you in the drawing room."

"Thank you, Mason." He glanced at the card, already knowing what it would say since he had been expecting Lady Crampton to arrive, and it appeared the woman was punctual. "Please ring for tea."

Mason bowed and left the room. Henry stood, rolled down his sleeves and shrugged into his jacket. During the short walk from his library to the drawing room, he looked once again at the card.

The Right Honble. The Viscountess Crampton
London, England

Henry was in dire need of a chaperone and companion for his two younger daughters. This year was Juliet's turn to marry—since he'd decided last year the girls marrying in their birth order would work quite well—and his lackadaisical chaperonage of Elise last year had ended with her marrying, already in a family way. Happily and much in love, but nevertheless, he hadn't done a proper job of watching over her.

What he needed was a stout, stern, ample-bodied woman who would guard his girls like a goaler and keep the rakes at bay with a mere glance. This one had been referred to him by Mrs. Benson, a lovely lady who had acted as chaperone for his girls on occasion.

He opened the door to the drawing room. His eyes widened at the sight of the beautiful woman in her prime—black as the night hair, creamy skin, and piercing blue eyes—standing right there in his drawing room. She could not have seen much more than thirty years. Her deep lavender morning gown fit her curves to perfection.

He felt a stir in his lower parts that he hadn't felt in a long while. Not that he'd been a monk since his dear wife passed on—it *had* been more than thirteen years—but no woman had caused such an immediate reaction in him since he'd buried Mary Margaret.

"Lady Crampton, I assume?" He walked farther into the room and waved at the settee near the window. "Please have a seat."

She sat on the edge of the settee, her shoulders straight, her back stiff, both of her gloved hands folded neatly in her lap on top of her cream-colored lace reticule. She regarded him with a poised, confident manner. He, on the other hand, felt like a youth chasing after the dairy maid. "I sent for tea."

She nodded, only making him feel even more foolish. Here he was, the potential employer, and she the prospective employee, yet he felt as though she were assessing him. Wishing he had thought to bring something to write with so he could appear as though he knew what he was doing, he cleared his throat. "I hope you had no trouble finding us?"

"No, not at all."

Her voice.

It fit her perfectly, and he found himself mesmerized by the tone. Not too deep to be sultry, but with enough depth and melody that he could listen to her talk for hours. "Yes. Well, then."

Thankfully, before he could appear even more ridiculous by stumbling over his words, the door opened, and Mason entered, carrying a tray with a tea pot, two cups and saucers, and an array of sweet and savory treats. The butler placed it on the table between them, bowed, and left the room.

"Would you pour, Lady Crampton?"

She seemed startled by his request. "Certainly. How do you like your tea, Lord Pomeroy?"

"Two lumps and a bit of cream."

She did as he bid as gracefully as he knew she would. Her delicate hands poured the tea, fixed it to his liking, and handed it to him. She then placed a few of the treats on a small plate and passed that to him.

After fixing her own tea and taking one small lemon tart, she took a sip of the liquid and then regarded him. "I am quite interested in your position, my lord. I don't know how much Lady Benson told you about my situation, so I think I should be honest with you from the start."

"Please do." He placed his tea cup on the table.

"I am a widow."

He dipped his head. "I am sorry for your loss, Lady Crampton. I didn't know your husband very well, but we did rub elbows in Parliament on occasion. That was quite some time ago."

"Yes. About seven years ago, Lord Crampton moved us all, him, myself and our two daughters, to his country estate where we remained until he passed away a few months ago. Once the new viscount took over the estate, my daughters and I came to London where we reside with an old family friend, Lady Penrose."

"I don't wish to be intrusive, but why are you seeking employment? Did Lord Crampton not make a provision for you?"

She hesitated and then shook her head. "Everything he left was entailed."

There was no need to push her further. Her hesitation told him there was more to it, but nevertheless, the scoundrel had obviously left his family in dire straits or Lady Crampton would not be seeking a position.

"Family?"

Again she shook her head. "No. In fact, his heir is a third cousin for whom my husband held no regard."

"I was not aware that you had two daughters. Their ages?"

Although he would have said it was impossible, her bright, motherly smile brought even more beauty to her face. "Yes, Lady Prudence and Lady Phoebe are twins. They are twelve years."

"Ah. Daughters. Lovely things. They make one's life fulfilling. I have three. One married, and two still to find their true loves."

"I assume they are the ladies you wish to hire a companion and chaperone for?"

He took a swallow of his tea, wishing it were brandy. He eyed the wretched little sandwiches

Cook had sent in and wondered again how he was still being served these ridiculous ladies' treats now that Elise had married and was most likely providing such sad fare for her husband. He must have a word with Cook and impress upon her that he wanted real food when tea trays were sent in.

"Yes, I had Lady Dearborn chaperone my darling daughters last Season, but I fear she fell short of her duties."

"I am sorry to hear that."

He perked up and smiled brightly. "Yes, well, the good news is I am to be a grandfather."

The poor woman had almost spit out her tea. He'd been amused at the slight blush rising from her neckline to her face at his casual words. A widow and mother herself, her discomfort at his forthright words was charming.

"C-c-congratulations." She dabbed her lovely lips with her serviette.

"Thank you. I do hope it's a boy."

He picked up a small sandwich of some sort of cheese spread and watercress, frowned, and dropped it on his plate. "I don't like this ladies' food." He brushed his hands and sat back.

"My dear wife passed onto her eternal reward"—he crossed himself—"about fourteen or so years ago. My wonderful daughter, Lady St. George—hard to get used to calling her that, don't you know—practically raised her sisters and did a fine job of running my household. Now that she has her own husband and home to apply her managing skills to," he grinned, "I need someone to look after Lady Juliet and Lady Marigold."

"My lord, I feel I would be quite adept in the role of companion and chaperone. I am, myself, a former young lady of the *ton*, and, as the mother of two daughters, I am more than qualified to deal with feminine matters."

"Yes, yes. I'm sure you are." He studied her for a moment, then stood, anxious to get the matter of her moving in settled.

She scrambled to stand as well, knocking the tea tray and dropping her serviette and reticule which had been on her lap to the floor. For some reason, she'd looked confused and flustered. "I am happy to have met you, my lord. I hope you find the perfect person to fill your position."

"I already have." Now he was confused.

She raised her chin. "I see." She picked up her reticule from the floor and moved toward the door.

Once she reached the entrance, she turned and offered her hand. "Thank you for your time, my lord."

"Good, good. I will send my carriage first thing in the morning."

Her jaw dropped. "What?"

"Is that too soon? I really would like to get you and your daughters settled before the Season starts."

"But I thought—"

He waved his hand. "No matter. Whatever your problem is, we can right it." He tapped his lips. "Although, it might take me some time to find a governess for your girls." He perked up and smiled. "That can be your first assignment."

The poor woman obviously had trouble following conversations because she stared at him with that confused look again. Nevertheless, she was the perfect companion and chaperone for his girls. And not hard to look at, either.

"A governess?"

He frowned. "Yes, of course."

"A governess is not necessary, my lord. I have rooms at Lady Penrose's home. If I am being offered this position, I can assure you my daughters will be well supervised there while I am taking care of your daughters."

"Nonsense. Girls belong with their mother. We have a fine nursery. I'll have my housekeeper, Mrs. Woolford, see that it's aired out and freshened up."

She opened and closed her mouth several times as though she wanted to say something but could not think of the words. Hopefully, her inability to hold normal conversations would not affect her dealing with the girls.

"I did not realize this position would require me to live here."

"Why not?

"I don't know, exactly. I'm not sure it is proper."

"Of course, it's proper. You are chaperoning my daughters, and I have a housekeeper, and soon your young girls' governess, who will chaperone you."

"You will have a chaperone for your chaperone?"

Ah, she was finally following the conversation. "Yes."

"I just assumed…"

Choosing to move forward and get her installed in the house to free him up from the burden of supervising Marigold and Juliet, he looked out the door the butler held open. "Did you arrive in your own carriage?"

She shook her head, still appearing a bit dazed. "No. I hired a hackney."

"Mason, see that my carriage is brought around."

"Yes, my lord."

"Now, I will send you home, but please be ready by, say, ten tomorrow morning."

She nodded and looked as though she were fighting female giggles. She was, indeed, a most charming woman.

"Good, good. I will have my precious girls ready to meet you once you arrive." He gave her a bow worthy of a queen and turned on his heel.

He returned to the library, poured himself a bit of brandy, and saluted his new freedom from chaperone duties.

CHAPTER THREE

Every item Selina directed the new lady's maid to pack was like a stab in her heart. She'd hired Jenny, with the solicitor's approval, in preparation for the girls' come-outs, along with a dancing master and finishing governess. She hated having to leave Pomeroy House, but there was no choice. If she were to uphold her reputation, she had to move back in with Lady Penrose.

She kept herself from completely falling apart by reminding herself that once the girls were married, she and Henry could marry. Clinging to that expectation kept the tears at bay. On the other hand, she had no intention of forcing Phoebe and Prudence to make quick matches just to allow her the freedom to direct her own life.

Henry.

Even though she hadn't even left the house yet, she already missed him. She loved him for his unique personality, kindness, and caring. As she helped the girls decide on which garments to take and which to donate to a worthy cause, she remembered when he'd first hired her.

She had been taken aback by Lord Pomeroy. Not sure exactly what she had expected, she'd certainly been surprised when the energetic man had strode through the door of his drawing room. He stopped so abruptly she had the desire to pat her hair and smooth her gown. The way he stared at her, she thought sometime was amiss.

As the father of three girls, one married and two ready for their Seasons, she had expected the typical rotund, slightly balding man who graced the ballrooms of the *ton* when their daughters had their come-outs.

Lord Pomeroy was none of these things. Quite tall, he made her feel like a small child. His wavy, dark brown hair with only a slight dusting of gray at the temples had been combed straight back, almost as if daring the curls to drop onto his forehead. Aging had certainly not affected his body in a detrimental manner. The man must have kept up his appointments at Gentleman Jackson's since his lithe frame filled out his jacket and pantaloons quite well.

It had taken her a bit of time to come to terms with the fact that the handsome gentleman who had entered the room was the girls' father and her potential employer. Finally, her heart had settled down and she took tea with him, pouring without mishap and acquitting herself quite well.

His strange way of telling her she'd been hired had rattled her somewhat, but she felt she had handled the interview quite well after she realized his way of speaking and how his thoughts ran through his head and out of his mouth.

She smiled. So many times in the four years she'd spent living under his roof she had to stop and just let his words replay in her head so she understood what he wanted. But she had no trouble loving him or knowing he loved her.

She'd been in his household for less than a year the first time he took her to bed. It had been the night of Juliet's wedding. She and Henry had been celebrating in the library with a final glass of champagne when they'd looked at each other and came together in a frenzy of passion.

Clothes flew everywhere, and it was pure luck that he'd had the presence of mind to stumble over the pantaloons puddled around his ankles to lock the library door. They'd made love by the fireplace. Twice. Remarkable for a man past his so-called prime.

Ever since that first time, he'd asked her to marry him at least once a month. Embarrassed at how poorly her husband had treated her, she danced around his proposals, and eventually they settled into a comfortable routine quite similar to married couples.

If only.

"Milady, Lord Pomeroy requests your presence in the library." Jenny entered the room carrying a large satchel and tried her best to hide her grin, which no doubt someone had told her was improper when dealing with her employer.

The girl reminded Selina of an elf. Small, red curly hair, freckles, and green eyes, she was right off the farm in Ireland but had trained for her position with Lady Penrose's lady's maid, and so far, Selina had found her to be quite competent.

"Thank you, Jenny." Selina swept past her and descended the stairs.

Henry stood as she entered the room, as did the man seated in front of the desk. "My lady, I would like to make known to you Mr. Jacob Barnes, who is my solicitor."

"Lady Crampton, it is my pleasure to meet you." Mr. Barnes bowed and offered a warm smile.

"Thank you, Mr. Barnes."

"If you will take a seat, Selina." Henry waved to the chair alongside Mr. Barnes. "I have been discussing your situation with Mr. Barnes to see if he is able to help us in any way."

If she didn't love the man so much and want to see a happy solution to her *situation*, she would have let Henry know how she felt about bringing his solicitor into her personal business without receiving her permission. But he only meant well, and she really would like to see what could be done. She merely nodded at the solicitor.

"My lady, I have no idea if there is a way to bring a happy conclusion to this matter, but I will need to begin by reviewing your late husband's will." He reached into a satchel sitting alongside him and pulled out papers. "This document will grant me permission to speak with your solicitor."

Selina huffed. "He is not *my* solicitor. He was my husband's man, and I have dealings with him only because the late Lord Crampton chose to name him as trustee of my daughters' funds."

Mr. Barnes nodded in sympathy but still held out his pen and the document. "If you will, my lady."

She signed and handed it back to him. As he folded the paper and placed it back in the satchel, he said, "I do not wish to give you unreasonable expectations. I am familiar with Mr. Darwin, the solicitor in question, and I have no reason to believe he would draw up a will that could be broken."

"I understand." Selina was quite sure of that herself. Crampton never did anything half-heartedly, and if he was so irascible as to leave her with nothing, he would be certain his wishes were carried out precisely as he commanded.

While theirs had not been a love match, he had grown ornerier as the years passed and no more children than the twins had arrived. However, she had no idea he harbored such dislike for her inability to produce another child. Fool her.

"If there is nothing else, I must excuse myself and continue on with our packing." She rose from her seat as did Henry and Mr. Barnes.

"There is no hurry, Selina. You can certainly spend one more night here."

Selina glanced at the solicitor who was busy shoving more papers into his satchel. The slight flush on his face told her he'd heard Henry's words and knew precisely what his statement meant. *Drat.* That would be the reaction of the entire *ton* if she didn't remove herself as quickly as possible.

"That is not necessary, my lord. We will be finished in plenty of time to have our things removed to Lady Penrose's home." She turned to Mr. Barnes. "Thank you for whatever assistance you can provide, sir."

He offered her a bow as she made a quick exit.

***

Later that afternoon, Lady Penrose's housekeeper, Mrs. Bloom, showed Selina and the girls to their rooms. Since they also had the newly employed finishing governess with them, the girls were given their own suite of rooms with a sitting room and a small room for Miss Fletcher. Jenny would be given a space in the servants' quarters.

"If you need anything, please have your maid summon us." Mrs. Bloom fussed around the already immaculate room assigned to the girls, checking for dust, moving a few items from their place to another place no different from where it originated.

"Thank you, Mrs. Bloom. This will be fine." Selina turned to the girls. "I will let Jenny help you get settled while I unpack."

"My lady, I will be happy to assist you once I am finished here." Jenny looked up from the trunk she was unpacking.

"No, but thank you, Jenny. I have no problem seeing after myself. You help the girls."

Selina left their chambers and walked the short distance down the corridor to her own bedchamber. It was a lovely spot, the same one she had before she'd moved into Henry's house.

Henry. Her heart hurt.

She shook off her melancholy and opened her trunk. Her clothing was sufficient, as Henry had insisted on her having a wardrobe appropriate for her role as companion and chaperone when she, Juliet, and Marigold attended *ton* functions. He considered it part of her salary, which she was certain, given what clothing cost, was much more than any chaperone had ever received.

Marigold's marriage might also put an end to her social events since women who had fallen low enough to seek employment were not generally sent invitations. She sighed and rubbed her temples. It had been quite pleasant to be part of the Season again. With Crampton's insistence that they remain in the country for the last several years, she'd begun to feel like a recluse.

Next year, Phoebe and Prudence would make their come-out and the social whirl would begin again for her. Parliament remained in session, with talk that it wouldn't end until August, so there would be more balls, routs, and garden parties. Would she be extended invitations?

A slight tap on her bedchamber door drew her attention. "Yes?"

One of the maids appeared at her door. "My lady, there is a gentleman caller for you. I placed him in the drawing room."

Henry? Her heart jumped.

"Thank you. I shall be down shortly." She pulled out one of her less wrinkled gowns and quickly changed. She did the best she could do with her hair and then smoothed the gown out and left the room.

She practically flew down the stairs like a young girl, then stopped herself. For heaven's sake, she'd only left his house a few hours ago. Adopting some dignity, she straightened her shoulders, put a warm smile on her lips, and opened the door.

"My lady! What a pleasure to see you again."

Lord Crampton.

Disappointment flooded her body, replacing the excitement she'd felt since the maid had announced a visitor. Drawing on all her well-tuned manners, she gave the man a slight dip and said, "How nice of you to call on me." She waved to the settee near the French doors. "Won't you have a seat, my lord?"

Crampton flicked the tails of his jacket back and sat. She took the chair opposite him, wondering what the man could want from her. "I thought you were in Greece."

He leaned back and rested his ankle on his knee. "Indeed, I was. Lovely place, Greece. You must go there some time."

She nodded her acknowledgement. "Would you care for me to call for refreshment, my lord?"

"No, no. Thank you. I will only be here for a short time."

Well, then.

"Is there something I can assist you with, my lord?" Suddenly she felt uncomfortable. The man was regarding her in a most peculiar way.

"Actually, I have come to ask something of you."

She waited. He regarded her coolly. "You are a most uncommonly attractive woman and one who I have always held in great regard."

Uh oh.

She remained silent, not wishing to play into whatever it was he had on his mind. She'd almost never been in the man's company since he'd spent the last few years out of the country. Once he'd heard the contents of the will, he left a steward in charge of the estate and took himself back to Greece. But he had a look about him that she'd seen before in other men. A look she was not happy with.

"I would like to pay you my addresses."

Oh, no.

CHAPTER FOUR

Robert, the Viscount Crampton, studied all the expressions that crossed Lady Crampton's face at his declaration. He had not planned on marrying so soon, but if he had to do that to get his hands on the fortune now locked up for the twins, he would.

He loved his life precisely the way it was. He loved the climate in Greece, hated the dreary weather in London. His mistress, Dominique, kept his bed warm and active. But the money he received from the two estates he'd inherited from his cursed cousin was not providing him with enough blunt to really enjoy life.

His plan was twofold. If he had no other choice, he would marry the woman, and the money would automatically come to him since she was not to remarry. However, he had no reason to believe she was that stupid. In fact, she'd just left her lover's house without marrying him.

The second plan was to destroy her name. He'd just paid a visit to the stiff-necked solicitor to see about taking over guardianship of the girls to get his hands on the money that way. There would be thousands of pounds he could fudge the records for that could go into his pockets.

The blasted man told him in no uncertain terms the likelihood of him taking custody from the twins' mother was nil. On the other hand, had she been caught stealing from the trust or deemed to be immoral, then he could apply to the Chancery Court for their guardianship.

He'd only spent one evening at White's to learn Lady Crampton had been living with Lord Pomeroy for the past four years as his daughters' companion and chaperone. Although a few smirked at that arrangement, the general consensus in the *ton* was Lady Crampton was aboveboard and would not have any sort of improper arrangement with Pomeroy. In addition, there apparently had been a governess in place the entire time Lady Crampton resided there, as well as the daughters, their lady's maid, and a staunch housekeeper to act as chaperones.

One look at Lady Crampton at the reading of the will, and he didn't believe it for one minute. The woman was younger than he'd thought, and beautiful. It was impossible that she and Pomeroy would be together day and night for four years without ending up in the same bed.

However, instead of trying to prove she'd been improper while living there, he'd decided starting his own rumors regarding her lack of morals might spur new speculation about her life the past few years.

"While I am flattered at your attention, my lord, I'm afraid I must decline your addresses. I am not in a position right now to marry." She glared at him. "As you well know after hearing the conditions of my husband's will."

"I understand. Of course I would never press you for something permanent until your lovely daughters were happily enjoying marital bliss."

No, she was certainly not stupid. She looked as though she'd like to toss the vase next to her at his head.

He worked up the best smile he could. "All I ask is for you to attend a few social events with me. You see, since I've arrived back in London, I have numerous invitations and am not familiar with my peers. I need introductions and had hoped you would consent to accompany me to a few engagements to assist me in easing my way into Society."

"With no idea of anything further?"

"Not if that is what you wish."

She nodded, and he breathed a sigh of relief. It would be much easier to ruin her reputation if she was with him. A scandalous waltz, a word dropped here, a comment murmured there. Yes, he could easily start enough rumors to have the gossip columns happy.

He slapped his hands on his thighs. "Wonderful. I have been invited to the

Wolversons' ball in two days. May I call for you at, say, ten o'clock?"

Although she still looked skeptical, she agreed. He took his leave, bouncing down the stairs with his plan now in action.

Selina watched Crampton as he left the house with his jaunty step. Something did not seem right about his request. Of course, he would know she could not marry until the girls were settled, but she got the impression that was not the main reason for his call. Instead of looking sorrowful at her rejection, he actually appeared relieved.

Then there was the invitation to accompany him to the Wolversons' ball. Most likely Henry had received an invitation as well, but he eschewed social events, spending most of the evening in the card room if he was forced to attend for some reason. At least by offering help in introducing Crampton to the *ton*, she would continue with a social life until the Season ended.

***

Two days later, Lord Crampton arrived at precisely ten o'clock. Most likely only a year or two younger than her, he was a nice-looking man and certainly spent a hefty coin on his clothing. His black jacket fit his body to perfection, and she doubted he'd needed any padding from his tailor. The dark red and black print waistcoat lent a bit of a rakish air to his look. Dark trousers and an expertly tied cravat finished off his outfit.

He extended his arm as she reached the Penrose entryway. "My lady, you look quite lovely this evening."

"Thank you." She accepted her wrap from the butler, Holmes, at the door and took Crampton's arm. The first thing she noticed was the lack of warmth she generally felt when she took Henry's arm. Also, although the scent of something spicy emanated from Crampton, he did not smell of the comforting aroma of bergamot, Henrys favorite soap.

Crampton was shorter than Henry and a bit stouter. Not that she needed all those reminders to miss Henry. In the two days since she'd left his house, she'd heard nothing from him. Of course, she knew not what she'd expected him to do. Serenade her from underneath her window? Chase her down on Bond Street and drag her into his carriage to ravish her?

She giggled at the idea of him doing just that.

"Ah, it seems you have amusing thoughts, my lady." Crampton settled on the seat across from her and tapped on the ceiling of the carriage. She didn't care for the way he looked at her but could not put her finger on why. Perhaps she just felt at odds attending a ball with a man other than Henry.

She waved him off. "No. Just something one

of my girls said." Hopefully, he would drop his questions since she had no intention of telling him what she really thought.

It took less than ten minutes to arrive at the Wolversons' townhouse, but fifteen minutes for the carriage to creep up the line and deposit them at the front of the house. A footman opened the door and bowed. "Good evening, my lord, my lady."

Crampton stepped out first then turned to assist her. It felt odd to be here at this event without Henry and no Marigold to watch over. She was such a delight to chaperone.

The butler called out their names, and she and Crampton descended the stairs. So began a great deal of comments behind fans, raising of quizzing glasses, and smirks. She felt the rise of heat from her middle to her face and then chastised herself for being so foolish.

Most likely announcing Lord Crampton and Lady Crampton threw the gathering into a frenzy. Perhaps attending with Crampton had not been such a good idea after all. She certainly didn't want to begin speculation as to their association.

They made their way through the crowd. Crampton led her to where Juliet and Elise stood chatting with their husbands, Lord St. George and Lord Hertford. Selina sighed with relief. At least she did not have to spend the entire evening with Crampton.

"Lady Crampton, so nice to see you." Juliet

gave her a hug and then stepped back so Elise could do the same.

"It is nice to be here." She noticed the glances between Juliet and Elise and again second-guessed her decision to accompany Crampton.

"Lord Crampton," St. George said, nodding in his direction. "I believe we were introduced at White's the other afternoon."

"Yes. Indeed we were."

Selina turned her attention to Elise and Juliet. "May I present to you the Marquess of Crampton?" She linked her arms through Juliet and Elise's. "These are the charming daughters of the Earl of Pomeroy, Lady St. George and Lady Hertford."

Crampton took their extended hands and bowed over them. His manners were impeccable and his demeanor pleasant, but she still felt uncomfortable. Perhaps she was building on her deceased husband's opinion of the man—which was never good—in how she was reacting to him

After the group conversed for a while, Crampton turned to her. "The music is starting up. May I request you to stand up with me, my lady?"

She groaned inwardly when she realized it was a waltz. Balls almost never began the evening with a waltz, but this one had. Not sure how to get out of it in a mannerly way, she nodded. "Yes, of course."

They received more speculative glances as they moved to the dance area. This had *definitely* not been a good idea. Perhaps once the dance had ended, she could escape to the ladies' retiring room with one of the girls and ask them to tell Lord Crampton that she had taken ill and returned home. Either Juliet or Elise could provide her with their carriage.

"My lord, you are holding me too close." The dance had barely started when the rascal pulled her into a turn and practically plastered her against him.

"My apologies, my lady, but we were about to collide with another couple." His banal expression did not fool her for one moment. "Perhaps once the dance has ended, you will introduce me to a few people? I would like to take up my seat in Parliament, and it would behoove me to know a few of those with whom I will be rubbing elbows, as it were."

There went her plan to escape to the retiring room and then home. But she had agreed to assist him in his endeavor to do the right thing. Except she had a very strong feeling he had no intention of doing the right thing.

Once the dance ended, he gripped her elbow as if he knew she planned to run. "May I offer you some lemonade?"

"Yes, thank you."

As they strolled along, he leaned in close to her ear. "Introduce me to some people."

When she looked up at him, he was grinning as if he'd said something naughty. Whatever was this man about?

He squeezed them past a group of people, again pulling her close, and once more bending to speak into her ear. The crowd was so noisy, however, she didn't hear what he said. At that point, she was beginning to have a headache.

The sooner she made him known to some people, the sooner she could fake not feeling well—although it was beginning to look as though that would not be a ruse after all—and go home.

The next hour was a nightmare. Based on his behavior, she was certain every person she'd introduced Lord Crampton to came away with the impression that there was more going on between the two of them than what really was. It was nothing that he said, but more in his innuendos and the way he kept clinging to her as if he were a small child afraid to be lost in the marketplace.

They had just walked off from a conversation with Lord Manford and Lord Stevens when there was a tug on her arm. She turned to face Elise and Juliet. "My lady, please join us in the ladies' retiring room." Juliet smiled at Lord Crampton. "Please excuse us, my lord, but there is an issue that we need Lady Crampton's assistance with."

CHAPTER FIVE

White's was unusually full for a mid-week afternoon as Henry handed his hat and cane to the doorman. He'd spent the last two days going over his accounts with his man of affairs and stewards from his estates who'd traveled at his request to London. Now that all the business had been taken care of, he could spend some time socializing.

He hadn't been all that sociable before Selina had entered his life, avoiding as many *ton* events as he could get away with, but she had encouraged him to visit his clubs more often and even attend a few evening *ton* events, which he'd done to keep her happy. Although, truth be known, he was more contented in the card room at balls and soirees, and since Selina was at the events to watch over his daughters, the plan worked quite well.

After requesting brandy from a footman, Henry joined a circle of men he'd known since Eton. Lords Melrose and Connors, and Mr. Rigby sat together near the billiard room. It amazed him how differently the four of them had aged. While Henry liked to think he kept his somewhat youthful figure due to his sessions at Gentleman Jackson's, Mr. Rigby had gone to fat. Melrose and Connors carried a couple of stones more, but the biggest difference was the lack of hair on Melrose's head and the perpetual scowl on Connors' face which had resulted in lines on his forehead.

"Have a seat, Pomeroy." Connors waved to an empty chair across from Rigby and Melrose. "We were just discussing you."

Henry accepted a glass from the footman and took a sip. "Indeed? I've been holed up with my stewards and man of affairs. What gossip could possibly involve me?"

"Actually, it wasn't you, as such, but Lady Crampton." Melrose placed his now empty glass on the table.

Luckily, Henry had not just taken a sip of brandy or most likely it would have landed in a wide spray on his lap. "Indeed?"

"Yes."

"What about Lady Crampton?"

"Word has it that now that she is no longer in your employ, she's looking for a protector. A couple of us were wondering if you have given her conge. She's a temptingly beautiful woman."

"What!?" A protector? His heart pounded in anger that her name would even be on anyone's lips in reference to such nonsense.

"No need to get your feathers in a kerfuffle, Pomeroy. Not necessarily a protector like an opera dancer might seek, but someone to help her along financially. Along with," Rigby winked, "certain benefits in return."

The roar that emanated from Henry's mouth shut down all conversation at the club as everyone turned in his direction. Completely unconcerned about the attention he was drawing for himself, he leaped across the table and grabbed Rigby by the throat. "Don't even think such a thing, let alone utter those words, or we will be choosing our seconds. The *lady* was in my employ as a companion and chaperone for my daughters."

Rigby looked at him wide-eyed, his face red from the pressure on his neck.

"Pomeroy, stop. You're going to choke him to death." Connors attempted to pull Henry off Rigby.

Henry released the man and stepped back. "I will do more than choke him to death." He turned to the other men in his circle. "Or to anyone else who has anything at all to say about Lady Crampton."

Melrose, the calm one in all circumstances, waved to a footman as conversation continued in the room. "A bottle of brandy, if you will."

"Pomeroy, even though it was never said, I have always thought you and Lady Crampton had an understanding. The fact that she moved out of

46

your house, it was assumed—maybe incorrectly—that the woman was available." Melrose poured them each a brandy from the bottle the footman brought.

"Available for what?" he growled, snatching up a glass.

Connors threw his hands up in front of him in a gesture of surrender. "Pomeroy, you must calm down and admit it was assumed you and Lady Crampton would marry one day, and instead of repeating your vows, she moved out of your home. You must admit that would raise speculation."

"What happens between Lady Crampton and myself is no one else's business."

"Come now. You know how the *ton* operates." Rigby poured brandy into his glass with a shaky hand. "There is always speculation and the thirst for a scandal or gossip."

"Now don't get all riled up again, Pomeroy, but the new Lord Crampton accompanied Lady Crampton to the Wolversons' ball last evening. From the way he acted, it appeared they were—for lack of a better word—cozy," Connors said.

Henry could no longer sit still. In fact, it would be best if he took a brisk walk to Gentleman Jackson's and beat the living hell out of someone. He would love to drag these three fools with him to wipe the smirks off their faces. Then he would make his way down the line to all the men unlucky enough to be at the salon.

He hopped up, knocking his glass of brandy to the floor. "Gentleman, I must attend to business." Before he quit the group, he turned and pointed his finger. "Do not repeat anything about Lady Crampton, or I will call you out." He waved his finger again. "All of you." Stepping over the now empty glass, he left the room, snatching his hat and cane from the doorman.

Halfway to Gentleman Jackson's, he remembered he'd arrived in his carriage. Cursing himself, he turned on his heel and made his way to the mews behind the club. "Lady Penrose's home," he shouted to his driver, who scrambled to jump from his perch and open the carriage door. Since Henry had no patience for such niceties, he pulled the door open, almost ripping it off the vehicle.

He tapped his fingers on his thigh as the carriage maneuvered through traffic to finally arrive in Mayfair. Henry banged on the ceiling of the carriage with his cane. "I will walk from here."

Once more before the driver could jump down, Henry had the door opened and was striding down the street, swinging his cane as if he were ready to beat anyone in his path. He raced up the steps to Lady Penrose's house and dropped the knocker on the door, a bit too enthusiastically.

"Lord Pomeroy calling on Lady Crampton." After uttering those words, he pushed past the butler the second he opened the door.

The butler gasped, wide-eyed. "I am sorry, my lord, but Lady Crampton is away from the house."

He shoved his belongings at the man. "Show me to the drawing room. I will wait."

***

"My lady, Lord Pomeroy awaits you in the drawing room." The butler at Lady Penrose's front door assisted Selina to remove her pelisse as she entered the house.

She had just arrived from a visit to Mr. Darwin, her deceased husband's solicitor, to outline for him all the expenses the girls would incur their first Season. Luckily, he did not question her on the things she requested, including a wardrobe for herself. He'd always been quite accommodating, although her contact with him had only started in the last year or so in preparation for the girls' come-out. Up until then, there was no need since she could not spend any of the money on herself.

It had always enraged her that her husband had his will set up in such a way that the girls could very well have starved or lived on the street until their seventeenth year. But then, Crampton had known she would provide for their daughters in any way she could. With some of the more seedy options open to someone in her position, Selina had been most grateful to Henry for the honest employment and home he'd provided for them.

She glanced into the mirror in the entrance hall and patted her hair. Her heart was pounding, her face flushed, and she felt like a young girl with her first beau. How foolish. But she had missed him dreadfully. Especially after having Crampton practically pawing at her the night before.

"Henry, how good of you to call." She burst into the drawing room, her hands extended.

He turned to her, and she sucked in a deep breath. He didn't look anywhere near as happy to see her as she was to see him. "Is something wrong, Henry? Is it one of the girls?"

"No. My daughters are fine, as I hope Prudence and Phoebe are." He bowed stiffly.

She sat and patted the space alongside her on the settee. "They are well, also. In fact I've just come from Mr. Darwin's office to discuss the funds that will be needed now and in the future for their come-out."

He nodded, his lips tight as he sat, but he left more space between them than she'd expected.

"What is wrong, Henry. I'm happy your daughters are fine, but there is something troubling you."

"How was the Wolversons' ball last evening?" The words barely made it past his stiff jaw.

"The ball? Just fine, I guess." She leaned her

head to one side. "Why do you ask?"

Henry jumped up and paced in front of her. "I was led to believe you attended the ball with Lord Crampton."

"Yessss." She dragged the word out. She did not like where this conversation seemed to be headed. Immediately, the same burning started in her stomach as when the deceased Lord Crampton had questioned her after each and every event. "Is there some sort of problem with that, Henry?"

He stopped and placed his hands on his hips. "I was told the two of you seemed quite 'cozy' at the ball."

Now she could no longer sit. She hopped up and faced Henry. Drat that Lord Crampton for making it appear they were more than just acquaintances when she was merely there with him to introduce him to members of the *ton*. "What exactly is it you are trying to say? Or accusing me of?"

"Nothing. I am merely repeating what I've heard."

"Gossip, Henry? You are now listening to gossip?"

He ran his fingers through his hair, then wrapped his arms around her, pulling her close. "I'm sorry, my love. Of course, you would not cozy up to Crampton." He dropped his arms and moved away from her, pacing once again. "However, this situation with you living here is causing talk."

She threw her hands out in a pleading manner. "Henry, I moved here to *avoid* talk."

Why, oh why, could she not be left alone? When Juliet and Elise had saved her from Crampton's clutches the night before, she was grateful, but then not so much when they arrived at the ladies' retiring room and the girls repeated the rumors that had been spreading throughout the ballroom.

The girls had also been distressed at her moving out of their father's home and had asked for an explanation. They, along with everyone else, it seemed, had expected a wedding to follow Marigold's. They both had planned to chastise their father until Selina had to finally tell them what the situation was.

Apparently, her association with Henry had been accepted by the *ton,* and now that she had moved out, it was assumed Henry had deemed her employment, as well as any romance, at an end.

No matter what she did, she would be condemned. Thought of as no more than a harlot if she remained in his home and a cast-off if she moved out.

Henry took her hand and led her back to the settee. "I am sure in a few days all will be well. I will accompany you to any event you are planning on attending. We must squelch any talk."

"That's the problem, Henry. I attended

events for the past four years as your daughters' chaperone and companion. As a rule, chaperones and companions are not invited to *ton* events. I had not received an invitation to the Wolversons' ball. Lord Crampton asked me to attend so I could introduce him to some of his peers." She sighed, remembering how frustrated she had been with him. "I must say it was a chore."

Henry perked up, his eyes boring into her. "How so? Did he annoy you in any way? Did he put his hands on you? I shall challenge him at Gentleman Jackson's."

Before she could answer, Stevens entered the drawing room. "My lady, you have another visitor."

Right behind the butler, before he could even move out of the way, Lord Crampton came barreling into the room. "My dear, how good to see you again." His brows rose as he took in Henry as he slowly rose from the settee.

"What an opportune moment, Crampton. I have a few things to discuss with you."

"Henry," Selina warned as she tugged at his hand.

CHAPTER SIX

Lord Crampton cursed under his breath. What poor timing for his visit to Lady Crampton. Although they'd never met, Crampton was sure the man who looked as though he would like to tear him limb from limb was Lord Pomeroy. He sighed. Some fancy footwork would be necessary to keep him whole and hardy and not limping when he left the house.

"Lady Crampton. Would you be so kind as to introduce me to your guest?"

"Yes, certainly." She hung onto Pomeroy's hand like a lifeline. "Lord Pomeroy, may I make known to you Lord Crampton?"

"Fine. We've been introduced. Now, I have a few things to say." Pomeroy shook off Lady Crampton's hand and moved forward. Despite the slight trickle of sweat that rolled down Crampton's back, he held his place.

"What is that?" He tried a smile, but Pomeroy was not having it.

The irate man stabbed his finger in the air, a bit too close to his face for comfort. "You are to stay as far away from Lady Crampton as possible. You will not escort her to any events, you will not speak to her if you both happen to be at the same affairs. You will not offer her rides in the park nor strolls along the Serpentine."

"Now, just a minute—"

"I am not finished. If you see her on the street, you are to cross over to the other side."

Lady Crampton gasped, her face flushed. "My lord, I believe you are being a bit high-handed."

"Stay out of this, Selina. This is between me and Crampton," he growled.

Crampton smiled inwardly. If he simply waited, it was quite possible Pomeroy would hang himself. It was obvious Lady Crampton was taking umbrage with her lover's attitude.

She placed her hands on her hips and leaned forward. "No, *my lord*, this is not between you and Lord Crampton. Believe it or not, I am part of this conversation. And I will not be pushed aside and treated like a wayward young girl."

Pomeroy was stupid enough to roll his eyes. "Of course, you are not a young girl, Selina. You are years past that state."

Another gasp. Crampton wanted to do a jig.

Lady Crampton drew herself up. He swore she grew several inches. "Henry, I believe it would be best if you left. You are apparently overwrought."

"Overwrought? Damn, woman, I am

furious." He waved in Crampton's direction. "Do you know what sort of mischief this man has been up to?" He took a deep breath. "Furthermore, men do not become 'overwrought.'"

"It seemed that way to me, Henry. Nevertheless, you seem to forget I am a grown woman—not in my dotage, either, as you might wont to point out—and I can handle my own affairs." She flushed. "I mean, my own problems."

Crampton felt like rolling on the floor and laughing. Left alone, these two would do more damage to their relationship than he had hoped to accomplish in weeks on his own.

"I am merely trying to protect your good name."

"There is nothing wrong with my name. It is as good now as it has always been." She sniffed and crossed her arms. "That is, it continues to be good. As it always was. My name. Well, actually not my name but Lord Crampton's name. Which is still mine."

Pomeroy hung his head and rubbed his eyes. "Of course it is, my dear. I didn't mean to imply anything else. However, as I mentioned earlier, moving out of my house raised another set of problems."

"I don't see why."

Crampton loved the back and forth and wished he had a comfortable seat and a glass of brandy to watch the show. He could only hope it would get better—or worse.

"You don't see why because you are a woman."

Bloody hell, the man was really stepping into it now. Crampton almost felt sorry for the bloke.

The fire coming from Lady Crampton's eyes could roast a pheasant. A very large pheasant. Twice.

"I see. Because I am a woman. An old woman, as you've pointed out. How very thoughtful of you to remind me because that is something I have obviously forgotten."

"No, no, my dear." Pomeroy looked around, as if he were hoping someone would step in and rescue him from his tongue.

"Don't you dare 'my dear' me."

"Selina, you are the one overwrought. Perhaps you should send for tea."

"Tea, Henry? Ha!" She marched across the room, grabbed a brandy bottle, and splashed some into a glass, then gulped the liquid down.

Crampton cringed.

Lady Crampton's eyes grew wide and began to tear up. She immediately dropped the glass and bent over, wrapping her arms around her middle, coughing.

Pomeroy hurried to her side, pounding her on the back. She waved her arms frantically. It was obvious to Crampton she wanted Pomeroy to stop, but the idiot kept it up until Lady

Crampton moved away and, glowering at him, headed for the door. "Good day, gentlemen. You may see your own way out."

She continued to cough as she bounded up the stairs to the next level.

Crampton turned to Pomeroy and saluted him. "Well done, my man."

***

Selina stomped up the stairs, mumbling to herself. How dare Henry be so arrogant! Not that she wanted to spend any time with Crampton, but to be told—and not even directly to her—that she could no longer associate with the man was beyond the pale. Cross the street, indeed!

Perhaps it was a good thing she was unable to marry him. If this is how he planned to behave when she legally belonged to him—how she hated that term, too—her life could become as miserable as it had been when she was married to Crampton.

Men! She'd had enough of them for one day. Maybe for the rest of the week, actually. Or her life.

"Mama, Miss Fletcher would like to take us for a stroll on Bond Street to see some of the shops. May we go?" Phoebe met her at the top of the stairs.

The new finishing governess was settling in quite nicely. She loved to accompany the girls on various treks, continuing lessons on conduct in public as they visited shops.

"Yes, of course. Be sure to take Jenny and a footman with you, as well."

"Did I hear Lord Pomeroy's voice downstairs just now?"

Selina wrapped her arm around her daughter and walked the corridor to her room. "Yes, he came for a short visit. He is gone now." Or he should be.

"Oh, I do miss him so much. I wish I had known."

Her girls had a wonderful relationship with Henry, who in turn treated them as if they were his own daughters. They had received more love and attention from Henry in the past four years than they'd had from their own father.

The blasted man. Both men, and men in general. Pompous arses that they were.

"He was in a bit of a hurry. But if you send him a note, I'm sure he will be happy to receive you and Prudence for tea one afternoon." She grinned, remembering how much Henry hated those little tea sandwiches. "Be sure and ask Cook for the little sandwiches that go with the tea."

"Thanks, Mama." Phoebe kissed her on the cheek and headed to her rooms.

***

The next afternoon Selina and a footman left the house to travel to Hatchard's, her favorite bookstore. It had been a while since she'd treated herself to a new book, but since she no longer had the use of Henry's library, now was a good time. Lady Penrose's library—if it could be called such—was quite lacking in interesting reading.

After two days of rain, the sky was a beautiful robin's egg blue with soft clouds occasionally blocking out the bright sun. With summer in full bloom, she looked forward to long walks in the park. Perhaps she and the girls could take a ride around the park one afternoon when all of Society was there to see and be seen. 'Twas a good way to introduce them to the *ton* in anticipation of their come-out the following Season.

Her spirits picked up as she entered the bookstore. The smell of paper and ink always excited her. What new adventures would she find between the pages?

"Good afternoon, Lady Crampton." Mr. Hatchard greeted her as she entered. He was a pleasant man, always willing to help her search for whatever it was she was looking for.

"Good afternoon, Mr. Hatchard. It is such a lovely day, is it not?"

"Yes, indeed. If I can be of assistance, please let me know."

Selina nodded and turned toward the stacks. She immediately went to the poetry shelves and began to peruse the titles.

"Selina." She turned at the whispered word. Henry stood behind her. "May I have a minute, please?"

Some of her anger at his prior behavior had diminished, but she didn't want to forgive him so easily. She was quite happy that he'd taken Crampton to task, but she still didn't care for the manner in which he'd treated her like she wasn't even present.

"I just arrived, Henry. I would like some time to browse."

"Fine. Then suppose I do some browsing myself, and when you are ready, we can take tea at Gunter's or any other tea shop you prefer?"

She really should deny his request, but he looked so pathetic, she could not do it. "Very well. But don't rush me."

Henry held his palms out. "No. Not at all. Take your time." He began to whistle as he moved to the history section.

Selina shook her head and continued to browse, pulling out a copy of *Graham Hamilton* by Lady Caroline Lamb.

***

Henry breathed a sigh of relief when Selina agreed to take tea with him. He'd only been gone from her house for about twenty minutes when he realized what a huge mistake he'd made and what an arse he'd been.

He blamed it all on Crampton, of course. The man had some sort of plan that involved Selina, he was sure. Once Crampton had accepted his title, he'd hurried back to Greece where he'd been for the past four years. Now he'd arrived in London, looking for introductions to his peers so he could take up his seat in Parliament. At least, that was his story. Henry didn't believe it for one minute.

Once Selina had left them in Lady Penrose's library, with the two men staring after her, Henry had turned to Crampton and waved toward the door. "This way out, Crampton."

The man had a rather nasty smirk on his face that Henry wished to remove, but being a gentleman and not wanting to make things worse with Selina, he ignored the gloat and left right behind Crampton.

After about thirty minutes, Selina approached him with two books in her arms. "I am ready to leave, Henry. Have you finished?"

"Yes. Indeed I have." He placed the book he'd been flipping through back on the shelf and followed Selina to the counter. Once Hatchard had advised Selina of the amount of her purchase, Henry withdrew his pouch and plunked the coins on the countertop.

"That isn't necessary. I can purchase my own books."

He took Selina by the elbow and steered her out of the store. "Consider it part of your salary."

She took his extended arm. "I am no longer in your employ."

"Well, I was about to give you a raise and you

left before I could advise you of that."

She laughed, and his heart lightened and his spirits rose. Nothing felt better than hearing Selina laugh. Well, perhaps there were one or two other things—most of them taking place between his sheets—but sunshine and a bright smile from Selina put his world back where things belonged.

With it being such a wonderful day, they walked the short distance from Hatchard's on Piccadilly to Gunter's on Berkeley Square. Thinking that having tea in front of them would make their conversation more pleasant, they spoke only about the weather, the bookstore, and the girls' note to Henry about stopping by for tea one day the following week.

"I do miss those girls, you know." Henry directed her past a young child causing trouble for his nanny. "Things are so quiet since you all left."

"Yes. It's been adjustment for us, as well. I told the girls to send you a note because they were feeling a bit despondent." She looked at him with a smirk. "For some reason, they seem to miss you."

"Ah, and you do not?"

Selina sniffed. "I'm not quite sure. It depends on who you truly are. I have had my doubts of late."

He frowned. "What does that mean?"

"Never mind. We are at the shop. Once we have our tea, we can resume our conversation."

Henry opened the door and bowed. "As you wish, my lady."

CHAPTER SEVEN

Gunter's was one of the more fashionable tea houses in London. They also served ices, which were quite popular with the *beau monde*. Many of the fashionable set spent time there after shopping or an afternoon ride in the park.

Since it was too early for most riders to be finished with their traverse around Hyde Park, there were only a few tables populated with customers. Henry held out a chair for Selina and joined her from across the table. A waiter immediately appeared, and they placed their orders.

"Selina, I wish to apologize for my behavior recently. I overreacted and placed you in a difficult position."

"Yes. Indeed, you did."

He tugged at his cravat. Normally, he eschewed the blasted thing—at least in his own home—but proper dress required it once a gentleman stepped out of his house. "I do not wish to distress you, but there has been speculation that the reason you moved out of my house was because we were no longer *involved*."

"That is preposterous, Henry. Everyone knows I could not stay in your house once Marigold married. It was even risky while your daughter was in residence. Instead of making something foul out of it, I should be applauded for doing the correct and proper thing."

"My dear, you know how the *ton* loves gossip and potential scandal."

Selina huffed. "I am certainly not of an age to create scandal."

The waiter arrived with their tea and sweets. He bowed and left them, and Selina poured, fixing his tea precisely as he liked it. Gads, he missed her for so many reasons.

"In any event, somehow word has reached my ear that you are looking for another—person—to…"

Her brows rose. "To what?"

"I hate to say this, but to warm your bed."

Both of her hands flew to her mouth, and her face flushed bright red. "Surely you are mistaken. I have never done anything to indicate I am that type of widow. I have always been respectable and conducted myself in a proper manner."

Henry glanced around at the few people in the tea house who looked with too much interest in their direction. "My dear, calm yourself. Of course, you have always been aware of the proprieties." He would be foolish, indeed, to mention that she'd warmed his bed for a couple of years, which was not exactly proper, but he'd always followed their romps in bed with a proposal.

Which she continuously and firmly refused.

"Why would someone say such a thing? I don't understand."

"That brings me back to Crampton." Henry wiped his mouth with a serviette and placed it alongside his plate. What they served here would only give him an appetite for real food which he would have to seek once he arrived home.

"Do you think he has something to do with this?"

"I am almost sure. He shows up in London after spending all his time in Greece, and suddenly he seeks you out to be introduced? He wants to take up his seat in Parliament? Not likely."

Selina blew out a deep breath. "What would be his purpose?"

"Easy. He wants to marry you so he can put his hands on the girls' fortune."

"Marry me! I would never marry that man. He is obnoxious, pushy, annoying, and he doesn't smell like you."

If his eyebrows could go any farther, they would fly off his face. "Doesn't smell like me?"

She grinned, and his heart melted. Damn, he had to do something to get her back into his house. His bed. His life. He reached across the table and placed his hand on hers. "We have to find a solution to this."

"Has there been any word from your solicitor?"

Henry pulled his hand back and slumped in his chair. "Yes. There is no way to break the will. As Barnes indicated when we met with him, Mr. Darwin is not one to make mistakes when it comes to legal matters. If you marry, the money automatically goes to Crampton. To my way of thinking, given how much your husband disliked his heir, I don't understand why he set it up this way."

"I'm afraid the reason he did that was he disliked me just as much."

Henry shook his head. "That is not possible."

"It is. In addition to always blaming me for only having girls and for not conceiving again, he moved us to the country because he kept accusing me of encouraging other men. He spent the last two years of his life dragging me from physician to physician for 'cures' for my inability to conceive." She shuddered. "Some of those 'treatments' were horrible."

Once again Henry wished Crampton was still alive so he could kill him. Slowly and painfully.

Selina continued. "I do want to warn you, however, that I will not pressure Prudence and Phoebe to marry just anyone so I may become free."

"No. I would not want that." Well, he did

wish for quick marriages for the girls, but he would not say so and cause another argument. And he truly wanted for them what his own daughters had. Love and happiness. "How is it you came to be married to Crampton? He must have been a few decades older than you."

"He was. I was eighteen in my first Season since we had been mourning the loss of my brother the year before. My parents never got over his death, and they wanted in the worse way to leave England and move to the continent where there were no memories of David.

"Crampton approached my father with an offer, money changed hands, and I was betrothed before my first Season ended."

His heart broke for the girl robbed of the things most young ladies looked forward to for most of their childhood. "Your experience was unpleasant, to say the least. I promise you a much happier life when we are married."

Selina dabbed at the corners of her eyes with her serviette. "I know, Henry. I know."

***

Two days after they reconciled at Gunter's Tea House, Selina dressed for a garden party at the home of Mr. and Mrs. Sanford, the third son of the Earl of Monroe. Sanford and his wife, a very young and flighty girl, had only married a few weeks prior and just now returned from their honeymoon. Their marriage was said to be a love match, although Selina could not fathom why the very stiff and staid Mr. Sanford had fallen in love with the silly Lady Marie.

She loved her pale blue muslin gown with a deep blue ribbon under her breasts and around the hem of the gown. She turned to view in the mirror how the ribbon tied into a lovely bow at her back, its ends flowing all the way to the hem. Although she'd worn this to several events, it remained her favorite, and she didn't care if one didn't seem fashionable, wearing the same garments. It was one of her favorite gowns, and she was looking forward to Henry's arrival to escort her.

The weather had been a bit threatening earlier in the day, but now the clouds had moved on and sunlight filtered through her bedchamber window. She was also excited because Prudence and Phoebe were attending with her and Henry.

Since the girls would make their come-outs next year, she thought it appropriate for them to attend a few smaller social events before then. Miss Fletcher would attend also so they would be well chaperoned.

"My lady, Lord Pomeroy has arrived and awaits you downstairs." Jenny peeked her head into the room, her arm covered with colorful brocade wraps.

"Thank you, Jenny. Are the girls ready?"

"Yes, my lady. They are just awaiting their wraps that needed a bit of pressing."

One more glance in the mirror to check her hair, and she left the room. Henry stood in the entrance hall conversing with Malcolm, Lady Penrose's butler. Both men turned as she descended the stairs.

"Good afternoon, my lady. You look stunning." Henry took her hand and kissed the back of it.

"Thank you, my lord. You look well yourself." Indeed, he did. His dark blue jacket fit his frame remarkably well. His buff breeches were tucked into well-polished black hessian boots, and despite his distaste for cravats, his had been folded in an extravagant way. Overall, his appearance was enough to set her heart to thumping.

"Is Lady Penrose attending with us?"

She pulled her gloves on. "No. She had an engagement elsewhere."

"Ah, here come the girls now." Henry's eyes lit up as Prudence and Phoebe made their way down the stairs.

As a proud mother, she thought the world of them, but even with a critical eye, she admitted they were quite pretty and would most likely have a very successful Season come next year.

They were dressed in similar gowns, white muslin with pink embroidered flowers scattered throughout the bottom of the gown and along the neckline, with yellow flowers decorating Phoebe's. Their straw bonnets were rimmed with flowers matching their gowns and wide satin identical ribbons tied under their chins. Miss Fletcher followed behind them, beaming at the girls. She was almost as proud as Selina was.

Henry bent over Phoebe's hand, then Prudence. "My ladies, you are looking splendid. I will spend most of my time chasing off the young bucks, I am sure."

The girls both blushed and attempted to hide their giggles, which they were not at all successful in doing.

Unbidden tears welled in Selina's eyes. These girls were her babies. They were not ready for marriage. How could she encourage them to select a gentleman at their young age merely to grant her the freedom to marry Henry?

They should have a few years to enjoy the balls and other events before they chose a husband. And she wanted love for her girls. Besotted husbands took very good care of their wives. No, even if it meant she had to put off her own happiness, it would be worth it to see her girls happily settled with doting husbands.

"Well, as I get to escort three beautiful women to the garden party, I consider myself the luckiest of men." With those words, Henry took Selina's arm, and they all descended the stairs to Henry's waiting carriage.

All five of them squeezed into Henry's coach. The girls were bubbling with excitement at attending their first *ton* event. Miss Fletcher reminded them of all the things she had covered with them. "I want to be sure you make an excellent first impression. Remember, you can only make one first impression."

The girls nodded, but it was apparent from their bland faces they had heard this sermon many times before. Selina leaned back and smiled. They would be just fine. They were pretty, with typical English creamy skin, intelligent, well-mannered, and well-trained.

Several carriages formed a line in front of them as they drew up to Sanford's house. Women wearing colorful afternoon gowns, clinging to gentlemen's arms, strolled up the pathway to the back garden, while footmen directed their carriages to the mews on the next street.

Henry stepped out once the footman let the steps down, turned and helped her, the girls, and Miss Fletcher. "I wish I had more arms," he said. "There are simply too many lovely ladies for me to escort."

The girls giggled again, which drew a sharp comment from Miss Fletcher. They followed the rest of the guests to the back garden.

The gardener had done a wonderful job of making everything look fresh and beautiful. The brick patio was lined with pots of flowers, and small round tables had been set out for the guests to enjoy the refreshments.

"I think I would like a stroll right now, Henry." Even though it hadn't been a long ride in the carriage, she was reluctant to sit again right away.

"Certainly, my dear." He extended his arm.

"I will stay with the girls," Miss Fletcher said.

She and Henry took the few steps down to the garden area and walked the pathway. "It is such a lovely afternoon, and the Sanford gardener has done a wonderful job." She pointed to her left. "Look at those beautiful roses!"

Their stroll took them around the garden, where they admired all the flowers, the pathway leading them back to the patio where many more guests had gathered. She felt Henry's arm stiffen under her hand. "What is it, Henry?"

"Crampton," he growled.

Selina looked up to where Phoebe and Prudence stood conversing with Lord Crampton, who was standing much too close to them. Miss Fletcher looked around, as if searching for someone. Most likely her and Henry.

CHAPTER EIGHT

Henry practically dragged Selina along as he made his way to the patio where that bounder, Lord Crampton, had the nerve to converse with the girls. "Here, Crampton, what are you doing?"

He turned swiftly, his eyes wide. Recovering quickly, Crampton bowed. "Pomeroy, Lady Crampton."

Henry hated the way the man said Selina's name, as if she belonged to him. His anger had him seeing red but scuffling on the patio of the Sanford home would not be acceptable behavior for a guest. "Girls, go with your mother and Miss Fletcher into the house for refreshments."

Prudence and Phoebe quickly departed with Miss Fletcher, but Selina, her shoulders stiff and her lips tight, didn't look as though she was going anywhere. Damn, why couldn't she just once do as he bid?

"What is your problem, Pomeroy? I was merely passing the time with *my cousin's daughters* at a garden party."

"The girls are no relation to you. Your

connection with the former Lord Crampton was so far removed a monkey in the wilds of Africa is closer. Just as I told you to stay away from Lady Crampton, I also warn you to avoid at all costs any contact with Lady Prudence and Lady Phoebe."

Crampton pulled on the cuffs of his jacket. "Is that right, Pomeroy? And what gives you the authority to dictate who the charming young ladies and my cousin's widow"—he grinned at Selina—"spend their time with? Perhaps I am mistaken, but I do not remember hearing of a wedding between the two of you. In fact, rumor has it that you threw her over and now she is seeking—"

Before the man even finished the sentence, Henry smashed him in the face. He flew backward, barely missing Lady Marion and her mother, Lady Smythe, and landed on his arse. Realizing what he'd just done and where he was, and the gasp coming from Selina, Henry said, "My apologies, Crampton. I must speak with Sanford about the loose brick you tripped over."

Crampton climbed to his feet and placed a handkerchief against his bloody nose. "You will pay for this, Pomeroy." He turned on his heel and left the patio.

Henry took Selina's elbow and escorted her back into the house.

Conversations on the patio resumed. At least he gave the crowd something different to talk about than whatever the latest *on dit* was.

"Whatever were you thinking, Henry? To hit a man at a garden party is simply not done." Selina's angry whisper did nothing to calm his racing heart from what Crampton had been about to say. Either Selina hadn't heard him, or she hadn't realized where he was going with that statement.

The man was trying to ruin Selina's reputation, and Henry could not understand why. Did Crampton think if she became so distraught at the rumors she would marry to stop the gossip, giving Crampton all the money? He wouldn't put it past the man. He was devious if nothing else.

"I apologize, Selina, I know I should not have hit him, but I will not have him aligning himself with gossip about you and spewing it in public."

She sighed. "I believe you have made an enemy of the man, and, if nothing else, your actions might have made it worse."

He looked around. "Where are the girls?"

"Over there." Selina pointed to Prudence and Phoebe speaking animatedly with two young gentlemen with Miss Fletcher looking on.

Henry narrowed his eyes. "Who are those young bucks?"

"Mr. Applegate, the Viscount Brennan's second son, and Lord Marlberry."

"Brennan? Is he Irish?"

"Yes, Henry, he's Irish." She sighed. "Is that

a problem?"

The tone in Selina's voice told him if it was a problem, another problem would descend upon his head. "No, not at all. I was just curious." He waited for a few moments, then said, "Let's take a stroll in that direction. I would like to meet the men. I mean, after all, Phoebe and Prudence aren't officially out yet, so I'm not sure they should be speaking to young men."

"Henry, for heaven's sake. Do you expect them to converse with the potted plants?"

He patted her hand on his arm and led her toward the group. Applegate and Marlberry, eh? He would have his man of affairs delve into the men's backgrounds. Can't be too careful, and all that.

The men bowed in their direction when they joined the gathering. Introductions were made, and Henry proceeded to study each gentleman to make sure they weren't standing too close to the girls. He maneuvered himself and Selina so they were between the men and the young ladies.

He ignored Selina's kick to his shin, although it was, admittedly, quite painful. What the devil sort of shoes was she wearing, anyway?

"Lord Pomeroy, what is your position on the Cruel Treatment of Cattle Act? Mr. Applegate and I were debating it earlier." Marlberry addressed him as if he were questioning a very old professor in class.

The Cruel Treatment of Cattle Act? Bloody

hell. He really should get up to speed on what Parliament was doing, but with Marigold's wedding and Selina deserting him for some twisted sense of propriety, he hadn't taken up his seat in a while. "Yes. Well, I was considering it myself, but I need more facts before I can voice an opinion."

As stupid as that sounded to his ears, and from the expression on Selina's face, she thought so as well, the two men nodded, accepting the answer. He would also have his man of affairs look into the young men's school records.

After another—very boring—two hours of insipid drinks, small sandwiches, and banal conversation, Selina finally announced it was time to depart. Now he could go home and relax in his library with a nice sized brandy and order Cook to provide some real food. Perhaps he could convince Selina to join him for dinner followed by a bit of dessert.

The sort of dessert that involved a bed.

***

Crampton examined his black and blue nose in the mirror and swore. Two days since Pomeroy had hit him, and he still couldn't be seen in public. He tried using some white powder the day before, but he ended up looking like a corpse.

Pomeroy would pay for what he'd done. The man should be locked up or at least not allowed to leave his house without a keeper.

His plan to apply for guardianship of the two girls was moving along, however. He made sure everywhere he went that he mentioned Lady Crampton was looking for a replacement in her bed since Pomeroy threw her over. Once her reputation was in shreds, he would have his solicitor apply for guardianship based on lack of morality charges.

He'd been playing with another idea that might work even better, and while it wouldn't give him complete control of the urchins and their money, it would still put a significant amount of blunt into his hands.

The dump he lived in was growing old. His coins had dwindled to where he owed numerous merchants in Greece and was slowly mounting bills in London since his arrival. The income from the estates was not enough to keep him in the lifestyle he wanted. When he suggested raising the tenants' rent to his steward, the man pointed out how difficult it would be for the farmers to pay additional money. He went on, it seemed forever, about the children going hungry.

Whatever trouble the tenants had with their offspring was not his problem. However, when he thought about a small child with a hungry belly, he relented. He did not want to be the cause of a child not getting proper meals. Even if he couldn't pay his tailor.

Who also had children to feed. He sighed. He had to find a way to get money.

He looked once again in the mirror. He was to meet friends at the Rose Room, the finest gambling hall in London, tonight, but with his nose looking as it did, he needed to stay home. Better than making up some story about getting boxed at Gentleman Jackson's. Most men knew he never stepped into the place.

Damn that Pomeroy.

***

Selina joined Marigold, recently returned from her honeymoon, Juliet, and Elise in the St. Clair ballroom. The ball was probably one of the few that were left of the Season, although there was talk that Parliament would be in session all the way until August this year. Those who generally left for the country in mid-July would most likely change their plans.

Henry had sent along a note that he would join her later in the evening since he would be attending Parliament. Those sessions went on well into the late hours. No doubt he decided to attend since he seemed to know nothing about the bill Mr. Applegate and Lord Marlberry spoke about at the garden party.

She gave Marigold a hug. "You are looking well, Marigold. How was your trip?"

"Wonderful. We visited several cities in Italy. Our most enjoyable visit was in Pisa, where we viewed the Museum of Human Anatomy, recently opened by Tommaso Biancini. They still call it

'The Anatomical Cabinet.' There were more than sixteen hundred specimens. We saw fetal skeletons, skulls, anatomical statues, prepared specimens, and wax models."

Elise fanned herself. "Oh, goodness. That sounds…horrible."

Marigold offered her a grin and shrugged. "Maybe to you, but to us it was a wonderful, exciting day."

"I have no idea how you came to be our sister." Juliet shuddered. "Surely someone snatched our Marigold out of her cradle shortly after her birth and placed you in her stead."

"Where are you husbands?" Selina looked around but did not see them.

"The bounders all took off for the card room the minute we arrived. It would serve them right if we all found other men to dance and flirt with." Juliet sniffed.

"Is Papa attending tonight?" Marigold asked.

"Later. He is at Parliament tonight." Selina wondered how much Marigold had been told by her sisters of her move from Henry's house and the rumors being spread about her. She did not let Henry know she was aware of what was being said. He had hinted at rumors when she'd defended her position in moving, but she'd heard much more since then.

After Henry's altercation with Crampton, she'd gone over what the vile man had said right before Henry planted him a facer. According to

Crampton, the entire *ton* thought she was one of those widows who bounced from bed to bed. That, in itself, was not scandalous behavior since there were many women in her position who did the same, but she was guardian of two young girls. Her behavior had to be above reproach.

Hopefully, she and Henry attending events together would quell that gossip. He had been right, though. It seemed while she lived there the gossip had been subtle, but once she did the right thing by moving out, it had become more pronounced.

She didn't think she was very wrong in considering Lord Crampton had something to do with that. Of course, the *beau monde* was well known for bouncing from one scandal to the next. All she had to do was wait until some young lady eloped, or broke her betrothal, or got caught in the dark in the arms of a rake. Then Selina and her minor issues would be forgotten.

"My lady, may I request you stand up with me?" Lord Natterfield approached her, taking her by surprise with her so involved in her own thoughts.

"Yes, of course, my lord." She took his extended arm, and they made their way to the dance floor. She'd known Natterfield since her come-out years ago. He had married twice, produced no children, and word had it he was looking for another—young—wife to give him the needed heir. Which certainly was not her, as

Henry so blithely pointed out the other day.

They stood across from each other in the line, and the music began. As they twirled around, Henry came into view, standing next to his daughters. She smiled brightly until she noticed him glaring in her direction.

CHAPTER NINE

Henry merely nodded as Juliet went on and on about her new settee. He was far too busy watching Selina dance with Natterfield to pay attention. Whatever was she doing? Didn't she know her behavior was under scrutiny with the entire *ton?*

Not that there was anything scandalous about dancing with a man, but she seemed to be enjoying it quite a bit more than she should. He'd also noticed Natterfield smiling like some sort of cabbage-headed idiot. Since it was well known throughout Society that he was looking for another—much younger—wife, why was he wasting his time with Selina?

"Papa, are you even listening to me?' Juliet's pout hadn't changed in twenty years. Bless her precious little heart.

"Of course, my lovely. I heard every word you said. Your new settee sounds absolutely wonderful. I must come by one day with Lady Crampton and see it."

Looking mollified, Juliet smiled and

continued on with how the drapes behind the settee would now have to be changed. It was no wonder their husbands escaped the ballroom the minute they arrived at these various events. If he didn't feel the need to keep Selina out of trouble, he would be there himself this very minute.

The thought no sooner crossed his mind when the music ended. "If you will excuse me, my darling daughters, I must have a word with Lady Crampton." He hurried off, pretending not to hear Elise remark to her sisters how sad it was that Papa and Lady Crampton could not marry.

Indeed! It was that blasted deceased husband of Selina's. If the man wasn't already dead, he would challenge him to a duel and have the satisfaction of killing him on a field of honor. He dismissed the fact that Selina would not be in the quandary she was in if the man was still alive. Logic had no place in his loathing of the man.

"My dear, you look quite flushed. Shall I escort you to the refreshment table?" He'd caught up with Selina just as Natterfield bowed over her hand and took his leave.

"Yes, thank you, my lord." She studied him as they wove their way through the throng. "Is something the matter, Henry? You appear somewhat disgruntled."

He patted her hand where it rested on his arm. "Not at all, my dear. I was merely admiring you on the dance floor. You looked so lovely out there with all the younger ladies. I wonder why

Natterfield would waste a dance on you?"

Bloody hell. Did he just say that? He felt her stiffen alongside him and begin to pull her hand back. He clamped his hand on top of hers. "My apologies, my love. That is not at all what I meant to say."

She lifted her chin and viewed him from under lowered lashes. Lovely, long, dark lashes. "And what is it you didn't mean to say?" It amazed him that ice crystals did not form from her breath.

Whatever fool thing I uttered that obviously has made you want to dump a glass of lemonade over my head.

He waved his hand. "Nothing at all, my dear. I was merely pontificating."

Her brows rose to her hairline. "Henry, did you visit the brandy bottle far too enthusiastically before you arrived this evening?"

"Of course not. I am fully aware of what I am doing."

"That was not the smartest answer, you know." She shook her head. "I will forgive the remark about a dance being wasted on me if you care to explain what you meant."

He took two glasses of lemonade from a footman and handed one to Selina. "What I expressed so poorly was my observation that Natterfield seemed to enjoy your company far too much while he admittedly is on the lookout for er, a—young—bride."

Apparently, that explanation did not ease her

distress because she slammed the lemonade glass down on the table, turned on her heel, and walked away from him. He gently placed his glass on the table, watched her storm off, and headed for the card room, a much safer place to be right now. Besides, he needed the company of his sons-in-law to add some balance after all these women.

An hour later, having lost some hands and winning others, he ended up no better or worse off than when he entered. As he strolled back into the ballroom, his attention was caught by Selina in deep conversation with Lord Mallory.

He headed straight for them.

"Mallory." His clipped greeting had both Selina and Mallory turning to him with surprise. Selina's slight smile encouraged him to step a bit closer to her.

She moved away.

He moved closer.

She glared at him.

He sighed and backed up.

"I was just telling Lady Crampton how very pleased I am that she continues to enjoy all our social events even though she is no longer chaperoning your daughters." Mallory grinned in Selina's direction. And winked!

"Is that right?" Henry's stomach muscles tightened as he pondered the various ways he could strangle Mallory and still maintain his status in Society. "Something in your eye, Mallory?"

"What?" He had the nerve to look confused. "I just wanted to point out that she is such a breath of fresh air."

"True. I do find it easier to breathe when I am around her ladyship." Henry turned to Selina. "May I escort you outside for another breath of fresh air?"

If the laugh Selina was desperately trying to swallow was any indication of her frame of mind, Henry was not in as much trouble has he'd thought. Pleased with himself when she placed her hand on his arm, he decided to be gracious. "I believe Lady Bowman is headed in your direction." He nodded behind Mallory.

The man glanced over his shoulder, made a quick bow, and disappeared into the crowd, away from the notorious marriage-minded mama and the daughter she dragged along with her.

***

"Henry, what is the matter with you tonight?" They had left the noise of the ballroom and the patio where numerous people were also taking the air and strolled down the pathway toward the flower garden.

She sighed as he took her hand in his. In another month or so, Henry would retire to the country as he did every year, leaving her behind. London would not be the same with him not here.

He led her to a stone bench under a large elm

tree, where they sat side-by-side. He raised her hand and kissed her knuckles. "I miss you, Selina. I want you back home."

She shook her head. "Your home is not my home. You know that." She pulled her hand free and stood, turning from his dejected expression, and gripped her middle. "I hate this, too, you know. This was not my choice." She turned back, extending her hands in a pleading manner. "Please understand."

He rose and pulled her into his arms, making her grateful for the darkness of the area where they stood. The last thing she needed was for someone to see them and start more rumors. "I have an idea." He gave her that familiar grin that told her silliness would most likely follow. "I will adopt two girls, and you can move back and chaperone them."

She laughed. "Henry, I have two girls of my own."

He tapped his chin. "Yes. True, that. Then I will adopt them."

She shook her head, loving him more each day. He was funny, caring, a bit eccentric, and all hers. "If it were my money, I would give it up in a minute, but I cannot deprive my daughters of what is rightfully theirs for my own benefit."

Henry pulled her against his chest and rested his chin on her head. "I know. I wouldn't want it any other way, either." Before she guessed what he was about, he shifted and cupped her face. He lowered his head and kissed her. Lightly at first, then with more passion then she would have preferred, given their surroundings.

"Come home with me." He scattered kisses on her eyelids, her nose, her chin, and back to her lips.

Even though it hadn't been that long, she felt as though it had been forever since he'd held her in his arms. The familiar scent of bergamot that always surrounded him drifted to her nose, tightening the muscles in her lower belly. She grew damp and warm, and pressed her lower parts against his thigh that somehow had found its way between her legs.

She pulled away, taking gulps of air. "Henry, we must stop this. If anyone should walk by…"

"I agree." He ran his fingers through his hair and reached out and took her hand. "Come home with me. How did you arrive?"

"Lady Penrose was gracious enough to lend me her carriage, but I sent the driver home once I arrived since she needed it. I knew one of the girls would see me home."

"*I* will always see you home." He tucked a loose curl behind her ear. "You must know that." His eyes studied every part of her face, as if he was seeing her for the first time.

Selina laughed to break the tension. "I'm not sure of that. I have a feeling if I stepped into your carriage, your driver would only remember where *your* home is."

"Good idea. Let's go to my house and have a drink." He placed his lips next to her ear. "I have a bottle of the best French brandy the smugglers could sell."

She pulled back. "Smugglers? You didn't!"

"Do you not see how low I have sunk? When you ran my household, there was never French brandy. Now I am inundated with all manner of illegal things."

She narrowed her eyes. "Such as?"

He wrapped his arm around her waist and moved her forward. "I am afraid you will have to see for yourself. 'Tis a short ride to Pomeroy House. It won't take much time at all."

Her mind screamed *Don't go*, but her body and her heart shouted their approval. While she continued to wrestle with her conflicting feelings, Henry had requested his carriage be brought around, and soon they were making their way down the stairs.

Once they were settled and Henry tapped on the roof to alert the driver they were ready to go, she said, "Perhaps you should ask the driver to go directly to Lady Penrose's house. I am not sure this is a good idea."

"Oh, my dear. I'm afraid this driver doesn't know London all that well. He would never find his way to anywhere but home. Once we arrive at my house, I can have this driver look for the footman who knows the other driver who might know how to find Lady Penrose."

"Indeed?" She couldn't help but smile at his nonsense.

"Yes. And since it will take some time to rouse the other driver—who usually retires quite early with his own bottle of spirits—you might as well have a little bit of the French brandy."

"I love you, Henry."

He reached across the space and pulled her onto his lap. "Why don't you move back—"

"Don't ruin the moment." She leaned forward and placed her lips on his.

CHAPTER TEN

Henry poured a glass of brandy for himself, and at her request, a sherry for Selina. He walked across the library and handed her the glass.

He took the seat alongside her and rested his arm on the back of the settee. He felt at peace for the first time since she'd packed up and left.

Selina took a sip of her drink and placed the glass on the low table in front of them. She turned toward Henry and took his hands in hers. "There is something I feel we must speak about."

"Yes. You may move back in anytime."

She smiled but placed her finger against his lips. "No, Henry. This is a serious matter."

"What is it, my love?"

"I know I told you how Crampton moved us to the country because he wanted an heir."

Henry nodded.

"He told me the reason for that was he didn't trust me. He questioned me after every ball about each man I danced with, spoke with, drank a lemonade with. You know how things are at these events. Most husbands escape to the card room immediately upon arrival and the women dance and gossip. I love to dance, and I imagine it shows on my face, so I was asked to stand up quite frequently." She took another sip of sherry.

A small niggle of guilt began to grow in his stomach. He had been a bit possessive and overbearing of late. "Go on."

"That same feeling of irritation at being condemned for something I had no intention of ever doing returned again tonight."

When he opened his mouth to respond, she shook her head. "You have never questioned me before as much as you have since our separation. I will not tolerate the same sort of husband Crampton was. I am an honorable woman. I would never forsake my vows, which is precisely why I feel fighting these rumors about me looking for a new man to warm my bed is so terribly unfair." Another sip. "I realize we are not married, but please understand I will never again marry someone who feels I cannot be trusted around other men."

Henry's heart stuttered and then sunk into his belly. Selina was right. He had never behaved in such a manner before. Did he actually believe the rumors? Of course not. He knew Selina better than any woman in his life. Including his deceased wife. He and Selina had a very strong relationship.

He'd been a cad.

"You are correct, my dear. I have been

somewhat accusatory, and for that I apologize. I know the type of person you are. I have faith in you and your behavior." He ran his finger down her soft cheek. "Will you forgive me?"

"You must mean it, Henry. As much as I love you, I will never consider marriage if I feel watched." She waved her finger at him. "And don't try to tell me I've changed since I removed myself to Lady Penrose's home."

"No. You have not changed. And whatever little bit of insecurity I've been feeling will have to be conquered."

"Thank you." She smiled at him over the rim of her glass. "Now that we have settled that issue, perhaps you can think of a way we can celebrate our understanding?"

The look in her eyes had his body humming. He downed the last of his brandy, stood, and held out his hand. "I have a number of methods to celebrate." He nodded at her hand. "Finish your drink, my lady."

Her eyes never left his as she swallowed the last of the liquid and took his hand. They made their way upstairs to his bedchamber. Since they oftentimes shared the same bed all night before one of them returned to their own room before daylight, his bed had seemed cold and impersonal since Selina had left. Having her here in his room made everything seem right again. Finished. Complete.

Like a long-time married couple, they

undressed each other with ease, Henry kissing her soft skin as each fastener opened. He took her hairpins out, one by one, dropping them on the small china dish next to her side of the bed. He closed his eyes as he nuzzled her neck, the light scent of something flowery teasing his senses.

Their clothes piled on the floor, Henry eased Selina down onto the bed, covering her body with his. He wanted very much to take his time, but her absence made that quite difficult. Because of his age, he couldn't look forward to more than one 'event' per evening, so this needed to be good.

He used all of his control to think of other things while he kissed her and touched, licked, and fondled all the parts of her body he knew gave her pleasure. "I am sorry, my love, but quite anxious to feel your moist warmth when we join."

She looked into his eyes and smoothed back the hair that had fallen over his forehead. "I'm ready, Henry. Take me."

"Ah, my love." He slid easily into her moistness. Passion was so much more when lovers were past the first bloom of youth. The familiar comfort of her body, the well-known sounds she made when he moved, the way her breathing increased when he knew she was close to climax. The strength of her legs as she wrapped them around his waist, her heels pressing into his buttocks.

He took her mouth in a searing kiss,

sweeping her mouth with his tongue, touching all the places he knew set her on fire. She responded in kind as he moved faster, eager and at the same time, reluctant to bring it all to completion.

With one final thrust, he poured himself into her at the same time her muscles tightened and contracted around his cock, milking him, taking his very essence into her body.

Selina felt as though all her bones had melted. Henry pushed himself off her and collapsed, panting as though he'd run a race. The sound of their heavy breathing and the scent of their sex filled the air. All she wanted to do at that point was curl up alongside Henry as they'd done for years and sleep.

But everything had changed. She had her daughters to think about. Her reputation affected their reputation. Not that other widows, and even married women of the *ton*, were not visiting various beds, but they did not live under the dictates of a monster of a deceased husband. It was as if he monitored her behavior from the grave.

She sighed and sat up. Henry gripped her elbow. "Don't leave."

"I have to. I will be fortunate if no one has seen me enter or will see me leave."

Henry rolled to his side and propped his head up on his hand. "Why? So many widows, in fact I would not be remiss in saying most widows, take lovers. I don't see them being held up to criticism. It is quite accepted."

"And they most likely do not have a man watching them from the grave. And, they are somewhat discreet. If I were to move back in here, discretion flies out the window. Remember, any sort of behavior is tolerated by Society as long it can be ignored. Except for young girls, of course." She stood and began to separate the garments in the pile by the bed into her clothing and Henry's clothing. "I have every reason to believe Crampton—not the dead one—is attempting to slander my reputation for nefarious purposes. Most likely having to do with money."

"I agree."

Selina rested one knee on the bed and regarded him. "That is why we have to be careful."

Henry sat up and twirled his finger in the air, and Selina turned around, holding her stays up while he fastened them in the back. So much of that they shared together was comforting. She felt much more married to Henry than she ever had with Crampton. While Henry was loving and tender, Crampton had been cold and unlikeable. Henry cared about her and her feelings; Crampton had stomped all over hers.

Henry had a distinct love for his daughters—even, to some degree, hers as well—where Crampton had ignored Phoebe and Prudence most of their lives. And now that hateful man was keeping her from having the love and fulfilling marriage that she and Henry could have.

"Stop thinking, Selina." Having finished lacing her up, Henry turned her and pulled her down to the bed. "We will work this out. I don't know how, but I do know I cannot wait years to make you my wife."

She patted his cheek. "If only, Henry. If only."

***

The next afternoon, Selina stood at the front door entrance and pulled on her gloves as she waited for Phoebe and Prudence to join her. They were headed to Lady Millerton's home for afternoon tea. A few outings such as this were good for the girls.

As she watched them descend the stairs, she couldn't help but think how young they were. At sixteen, they were still little girls to her. But in two months they would reach their seventeenth year and, according to Society, they were ready for the marriage mart. She shook her head. Look what being a young bride had done for her.

However, she would marry Crampton all over again in order to have the wonderful, lovely girls who made their way downstairs, followed by Miss Fletcher. "Girls, you look beautiful!" Were she a man, her chest would be puffed up.

"Thank you, Mama." They both spoke at the

same time, looked at each other, and burst into giggles.

"Now, girls. Do remember not to giggle when out in Society. I don't think you should adopt the bored mien so many of the young ladies do so they fit in, but just be your wonderful, lively selves and you will do just fine." She nodded to the butler at the door. "We are ready."

"Will there be any gentlemen there?" Prudence wanted to know.

"Yes. I am sure of it. There generally are, usually those among the group who are searching for wives this Season." As they settled into the seats, she gave them a quelling look. "You are both much too young to be thinking along those lines."

"But Mama," Phoebe said as she adjusted her skirts, "I thought the idea of a Season was to look for a husband. And it's only several months before our come-out."

Selina shook her head. "No, my dearest. You are only sixteen. Barely out of the schoolroom. Besides, you don't want to rush into marriage. You may find that no one appeals to you in that manner. Having more than one Season is not alarming, you know."

"Well, everyone will say we're on the shelf," Prudence said.

"No. You will not be on the shelf after one year. Please don't rush into anything. Marriage is for the rest of your life. You want to make sure it is to the right man."

"Papa wasn't the right man for you, was he, Mama?" Phoebe's soft words hurt her heart. She hated that her girls knew how unhappy she'd been when Crampton had been alive.

"No. I am sorry to say, it was not a good match." She tried to keep the sadness out of her voice, if only because the man was the girls' father.

"Yet you married your first Season." Rather than being accusatory, Prudence's words were more curious.

"Yes. But I had no choice. Your grandfather arranged the match with Lord Crampton, and he wanted a short betrothal."

After a few minutes of uncomfortable silence, Phoebe patted her hand. "I'm sorry, Mama." Then she brightened. "But you have Lord Pomeroy." Then she sat back and frowned. "Why don't you marry him?"

CHAPTER ELEVEN

Lord Crampton studied the old viscount's twin girls drinking tea with their mother at the Millertons' tea party. He was bored beyond belief and bloody annoyed at the young chits who kept batting their eyelashes at him and dropping their handkerchiefs in front of him.

Every girl was looking for a title, and even though he was almost an unknown among the upper crust, the mere idea that a young viscount was in their midst and unmarried was enough to drive the marriage-minded mamas hysterical with glee. He sighed. He couldn't wait to get his hands on Crampton's money and hie it back to Greece.

He knew as a viscount, he must secure his title and marry one of these giggling, blushing, annoying creatures, but not for a few more years. Then he would get her with child, banish her to the country, and go about his life as he wished. With any luck, the woman he ended up leg-shackled to would not be too hard to look at so he could do the deed without all the candles extinguished.

Crampton's daughters did not seem to be as annoying as the other chits at the gathering. They spoke softly, didn't bat their eyelashes, and even their blushes were not irritating.

Lady Bellamy approached with her daughter in tow. The girl was unfortunately cursed with a rather large nose and a missing chin. However, he bowed in their direction and prepared himself to hold onto a pleasant smile while the mother raved about the girl's accomplishments while the young gal stared at her feet and appeared to be wishing herself on the other side of the earth.

His mind immediately began to wander to his meeting the day before with Crampton's solicitor. Even though he'd presented the man with various streams of gossip about Lady Crampton's behavior, the ninnyhammer was unimpressed and told him in no uncertain terms that if he applied to the courts for guardianship of the girls, he would most assuredly lose.

It appeared his alternate plan would be the next step. When he realized the stream of conversation had ended, he glanced at Lady Bellamy who regarded him expectantly. Bloody hell, she must have asked him a question.

"I am sorry, my lady, but I'm afraid I missed that."

She tittered. Actually tittered! "That is quite all right, my lord. I just asked if you would be so kind as to join us for tea one afternoon."

Tea? If he drank any more tea he would float back to Greece. "I would be delighted."

Mother beamed, daughter blushed so red Crampton was afraid she would set her hair on fire. He bowed in their direction. "If you will excuse me, madam, I believe I am wanted across the room."

He hurried past other mamas who tried to stop him and made his way to Lady Crampton and the twin girls. "Good afternoon, ladies."

"My lord." Lady Crampton's greeting, while not exactly warm, was at least polite.

He beamed at the girls. "I am quite pleased to see you once again." He turned toward Lady Crampton. "In your mother's company, of course."

She eyed him carefully, no doubt Pomeroy's threat to leave the girls alone fresh in her mind. Unlike Pomeroy, she would not make a scene at a party, however. Too well-mannered.

He tilted his head to study them. "I must admit to having a difficult time telling you apart."

Lady Crampton touched the girl closest to her on the arm. "This is Lady Prudence, and her sister Lady Phoebe."

The girls made a delightful, perfect curtsy and smiled brightly. He mentally rubbed his hands together. Yes, this was a very good plan.

***

Henry wandered his library at a loss of what to do

with himself. The house was so blasted empty with Marigold married and Selina and her daughters gone. He stared out the window and reflected on how anxious he'd been to get his daughters married that he even made up the rule that they could only marry in order of their birth.

Elise had been the one he most wanted to see settled. He didn't mind how she was running his life, but in all honesty, he did want her married and settled. A parent always desired to see their children settled in life for when the parent departed this earth. Even though Elise had been happy with her spinster status, she was a much happier wife and mother. Not quite so edgy and quick to take offense. Content with a man to direct and children to raise.

"My lord, you have a visitor." Mason stood at the entrance to the library, a card in his hand.

Henry reached the man and took the card.

Mr. Ebenezer Darwin, Solicitor
London, England

"Show Mr. Darwin in, and send for tea." Henry walked to his desk and settled into the chair. He couldn't imagine why Crampton's solicitor would be visiting him.

Henry stood as the man entered. "Please, Mr. Darwin, have a seat."

The older gentleman sat at the edge of the chair, clutching a satchel to his chest. "I apologize for interrupting your day, my lord, but something has come up that I feel needs to be brought to your attention."

Henry nodded for the man to continue.

"I tried to contact Lady Crampton first, but she was not at home. Since I know you two are"—he coughed—"quite close, I wanted to do my duty as quickly as possible."

While Henry was digesting those puzzling words, Mason returned with a tea tray. As the butler laid out the tea things, along with the substantial sandwiches he had instructed Cook to send whenever he requested tea, Darwin remained silent but obviously on edge.

Once Mason had poured the tea and the men served themselves, Darwin took a sip of liquid and placed the cup in the saucer. "My lord, my concern lies with Lord Crampton."

"I assume you are not referring to the dead one."

Darwin almost spit out his tea and looked quite taken aback. Henry didn't know why since he thought that a reasonable question.

The solicitor wiped his mouth with the serviette and placed it alongside his saucer. "No, my lord. The very much alive Lord Crampton."

"Go on." The sandwich he just took a bite of was wonderful. Thick bread, several slices of beef, and a horseradish type of sauce that Cook made. Delicious.

"Lord Crampton visited my offices quite

recently. He tried, I might add unsuccessfully, to explain to me why he should petition the Chancery Court to obtain guardianship of Lady Crampton's daughters."

Henry sucked in a breath.

"Yes. I agree. I have no reason to believe he would prevail in such a petition. He tried to offer as reason Lady Crampton's reputation as immoral."

Henry growled, and Mr. Darwin's eyes grew wide.

"I am quite certain whatever rumors the man quoted to me were started by him. I will tell you this, my lord. The former Lord Crampton was a difficult man. As my client, I cannot reveal any confidential information, but I will speak to my discomfort on how he executed his will. But, as his solicitor, I had to do as he wished and probate the will as he had stated.

"I find the new Lord Crampton if not equally difficult, at least somewhat so. His unreasonable demands at the reading of the will set me on edge. I was quite happy when he returned to Greece and placed his stewards in charge of his properties." He leaned forward, tension in his body. "I must impress upon you that the man is up to no good. Watch out for Lady Crampton."

"Have no fear in that regard, sir. I intend to make Lady Crampton my wife, but as you know she would forfeit her daughters' inheritance if she did so."

Darwin shook his head. "A very unpleasant situation. But please be assured, Lord Crampton must be watched."

They both turned as Selina burst into the room.

***

Lord Crampton watched from across the street as Lady Phoebe and Lady Prudence went from shop to shop, their maid and a footman trailing behind them. This was the third day in a row he'd followed them as they wandered about town as he waited for the right time to put his plan into action.

How the bloody hell many clothes did they need?

Finally! After leaving a millinery, they both strolled arm-in-arm and settled in seats at a table in front of Gunter's Tea Shop. The maid and footman stood about twenty feet away, chatting.

Crampton strode across the street and slowed his pace as he approached their table. No need to cause alarm to anyone. "Good afternoon, ladies." He offered a bow.

The girls looked up at him in surprise, then responded with a slight smile. "Lord Crampton. Good afternoon to you, too."

He waved to a chair. "May I join you?"

"Yes," one of the girls said. "Please do."

Ah, good manners. Exactly what he had expected. "Have you ordered yet?"

"No." One young lady looked around just as a server approached their table. They placed their orders for ices, and the man wandered off.

"I must admit, I have a very difficult time telling one of you from the other." He turned to the girl on his right. "Who are you?"

She giggled. "I am Lady Phoebe."

"Ah, yes." He glanced over at the other girl. "Then you must be Lady Prudence.

She blushed and nodded, casting her eyes to her lap. Hmm, she seemed more subdued than Lady Phoebe.

"How is your lovely mother? She is not with you today?" He offered them a warm smile, knowing full well Lady Crampton rarely accompanied them on their afternoon stroll around town. Hopefully, their harridan mother hadn't said too many horrible things about him that they would chase him off.

"Mama is fine. She spends a lot of time in the afternoon catching up on correspondence."

"And you both enjoy shopping," he teased, trying very hard to be seen as the endearing older male relative. An uncle, brother, cousin. Anything to make them trust him.

Their ices arrived, and they chatted about the weather, the end of the Season, and how they would make their come-outs the following year. It was bearable speaking with them since they were not of the simpering, giggling, gushing type. Their maturity was remarkable.

The entire time he was fully aware of the maid who had stopped speaking with the footman and watched her charges with diligence. The girls might be trusting, but it was obvious the maid was not.

Once they had finished their ices, the girls seemed to grow restless.

He wiped his mouth and adopted a pleasant expression. "May I escort you to your carriage?"

Lady Phoebe nodded and began to rise when her sister placed her hand on her arm. "I think we should visit that last shop we were considering."

The girl looked puzzled. "What shop?"

Lady Prudence blushed. "You remember, sister. The one where we said we would return."

"I am not sure what you mean. I don't remember saying we would return to another store. We decided to take ices before we left for home."

It appeared Lady Prudence was more cautious than her sister. He had to assuage the urchin's fears, or he'd have to carry out his plan another day. "Please, do not let me interrupt your day. If you were planning on more shopping, then I would be happy to accompany you to the store and see you home."

"Lead the way, sister, since I don't remember which store you refer to." Lady Phoebe waved in the general direction of the row of shops.

"Um, on second thought, I believe I was wrong." Lady Prudence blushed again. "I guess we are ready to depart for home."

He extended his arms and both girls placed their hands there. He kept up a lively chatter until Lady Prudence seemed to relax, as did the maid and footman following them who had resumed their conversation.

Once they left the busiest part of the area, he stopped. "Shall we send your footman to summon the carriage?"

"Yes, of course." Lady Phoebe turned. "Marshall, please have the carriage brought here."

"Yes, my lady." He strode away from them, and Crampton discreetly beckoned his driver who waited at the end of the block. He kept the girls busy exclaiming over all the ribbons and other fripperies they'd bought that day.

Once his carriage had rolled to a slow stop right next to them, Crampton opened the door. With one quick movement, he grabbed Lady Phoebe around the waist and lifted her. "In you go." He shoved her into the carriage, jumped in behind her, slammed the door shut, and shouted at the driver, who pulled away at a rapid pace.

Leaving Lady Prudence and the maid staring after them open-mouthed.

CHAPTER TWELVE

Selina awoke from her nap feeling sluggish instead of revived. She had no idea what was wrong with her, but ever since she moved out of Henry's house she had not felt well. Upon awakening each morning, she eyed the cold spot where Henry should be, and her stomach churned as she fought the need to run to the chamber pot.

She oftentimes skipped her morning tea, just not able to swallow it. It was difficult for her to keep her eyes open past luncheon, and instead of accompanying the girls on their shopping treks, made up an excuse about taking care of correspondence when she was actually crawling into bed for a nap.

This malaise that had overtaken her had to cease. She could not marry Henry until the girls were wed and settled with their rightful inheritance. They were young and deserved the chance to marry someone who loved and cherished them. She did not want for her daughters the type of marriage she'd been forced to endure. If that meant she had to put her hopes and dreams aside, then that was the way of it.

She sat up and swung her legs over the edge of the bed and grasped the mattress at the lightheadedness that swept over her. *Selina, behave yourself. Stop acting like a child and get on with your life.*

She eased out of bed and rang for Jenny. Within minutes, one of the younger maids entered after tapping on her door. "I'm sorry, my lady, but Jenny is off with the girls, shopping. What can I do for you?"

"Yes. I forgot about that. Please have tea set up in the drawing room. I'm not expecting company, but I need to rouse myself." As the girl turned to go, she said, "Before you leave, can you please help me with my gown?"

The girl moved behind her and tightened her stays and fastened her gown. "Would you like me to fix your hair, my lady?"

"No. I can do that myself. And thank you."

The girl curtsied and left the room. Selina stared at herself in the mirror, and her spirits sagged. She looked terrible. Dark circles under her eyes, her hair listless, and she was quite pale. Even the very light freckles across her nose stood out like dots of dark chocolate. She dropped the brush onto the table and covered her face with her palms. After a minute, she lifted her head and looked again in the mirror, shocked when tears flooded her eyes and rolled down her cheeks. Whatever was wrong with her?

"Mama!" Her heart thumped, and she swung around as Prudence raced into the room, her eyes wide, tears streaming down her face. Her bonnet had come off her head and dangled behind her, bouncing against her back as she hurried toward her. "He took her!"

Selina jumped up and grabbed Prudence by her upper arms. "Calm down, Prudence. What are you talking about? Where's Phoebe?"

"That's it, Mama. He took her. He took Phoebe!" Her daughter collapsed onto the bed in a heap and wailed.

"Prudence!" she snapped. "Compose yourself and tell me what happened!"

Jenny flew through the door, wringing her hands. "Oh, my lady. I am so sorry. I was not paying attention like I should have been."

Selina's head pounded, and although she had no idea what had happened, her stomach muscles twisted and her mouth dried up with fear. "Jenny, please, you must quiet down and tell me what happened."

Between apologies, hand wringing, and swiping tears from her face, the girl told her how they'd met Lord Crampton at Gunter's and how he pretended to walk the girls to their carriage before suddenly opening the door to another carriage, throwing Phoebe in before climbing in after her, and instructing the driver to go.

"Oh, my God." Why would he want Phoebe? She had no money to pay for a ransom, if that was his thinking. Selina could think of only one thing to do. "I must go see Henry—I mean, Lord Pomeroy. Have the carriage brought around. Immediately!"

No longer concerned at how poorly she felt and looked, she raced out of the bedchamber door and down the stairs. After leaving a note for Lady Penrose, who was making her afternoon calls, she shrugged into her pelisse, pulled on her gloves, and ran toward the carriage, still tying the ribbons on her bonnet. "Lord Pomeroy's house. And hurry."

She fought down the returning nausea and tried very hard to ignore her headache, which was growing with every turn of the carriage wheels. It seemed to take forever to reach Henry's house, but once she was close, she jumped from the carriage, stumbling to her knees. Ignoring the burst of pain in her knees and how she must appear to people on the street, she limped up the steps and pounded on the door.

Mason opened the door and bowed. One look at Selina's face, however, and he stepped back. "His lordship is in the library."

"Thank you," she mumbled as she hobbled past him to the library. She burst into the room, at first not seeing Mr. Darwin seated in front of Henry's desk. "Henry! Phoebe's been kidnapped."

The words were no sooner out of her mouth than her knees buckled, and she slumped toward the ground.

"Selina!"

Henry caught Selina just before she hit the floor. "Mason!"

The butler had entered right after Selina and stood agog, for once his stoic countenance gone. "My lord. What can I do?"

"Have Mrs. Woolford bring a pan of cool water and a cloth." He took Selina's reticule off her wrist and riffled through it, looking for a vinaigrette. Not surprisingly, she did not carry one. He looked up to see Jenny standing there, staring at Selina. "Jenny, go to the kitchen and ask Cook for some vinegar."

Next, Prudence hurried into the library. "Oh, goodness. Is Mama all right?

"She will be. In a minute." He picked Selina up and strode to the settee, laying her gently down. She looked so very pale. And as though she'd lost weight. Even though he'd seen her recently, he hadn't noticed how much she'd changed since she left him.

Jenny and Mrs. Woolford entered the room together with Cook and another maid. "Oh, my. What has happened to her ladyship?" Mrs. Woolford asked as she handed the pan of water and cloth to Henry.

"I don't have a lot of information right now." He turned to Jenny and Prudence. "Can someone please tell me what happened?"

As they both spoke at the same time, not making any sense at all, he swiped the vinegar under Selina's nose, which caused her to move her head aside and cough. He tapped her cheek. "Selina, wake up."

Her eyelids fluttered open and she frowned. "What happened?" Then she sat up abruptly. "Phoebe."

Henry reached out and touched her shoulder. "I am just now hoping to get some information, but I think you should lie down for a while."

"I can't. I have to find my daughter."

The poor woman looked dreadful as tears ran down her pale cheeks. He looked around the room. "Darwin, Phoebe, Jenny, all of you take a seat. The rest of you can return to your duties."

After a great deal of shuffling and murmuring, the room quieted down with Prudence and Selina sniffing into handkerchiefs. Despite how it looked to everyone else in the room, he sat next to Selina and pulled her against him so her back rested on his chest. "Prudence, in a calm voice, please tell me what happened."

"Lord Crampton kidnapped Phoebe."

Well, then. The girl certainly knew how to come to the point. "Thank you. How did he take her?"

"We were walking away from Gunter's with him, and his carriage pulled up alongside us and he opened the door, picked up Phoebe, and tossed her into the carriage. Before either Jenny or I could say a word, he hopped in after her and the carriage pulled away."

Henry closed his eyes and pinched the bridge of his nose. "Before we go any further with this, I want you all to understand that Crampton will not harm Phoebe."

Selina turned to him, the tip of her nose red. "How do you know that? He is a despicable man."

"Because he wants money. In addition to being despicable, he is a blackguard who would gain nothing by doing Phoebe physical harm."

"I hear a 'but' in there," Selina said.

Henry looked over at Darwin. "The will was written so the only way Crampton would get his hands on the money was if Lady Crampton married."

"That is correct, my lord."

"But if he married one of the girls, he would gain their portion of the inheritance, which I assume is considerable."

Darwin's mouthed dropped open and he nodded. "Yes. Indeed. As her husband, he would have unlimited rights to her money."

Henry looked down at Selina. "There you have it. He has kidnapped Phoebe with a plan not to harm her, but to marry her."

"My sister would never marry a man who kidnapped her!" Prudence gasped.

"If his actions come to light, she will be

ruined, and she would have no choice but to marry him." Selina's words were barely above a whisper.

Henry shifted Selina so she sat against the settee and he stood. He held out his hand. "Come. We are going to Crampton's house."

"Why? You don't think he was foolish enough to bring her there, do you?" Selina asked.

"No. I don't think that at all, but with his man driving off with Phoebe obviously being taken against her will, there might be others in his household who knew something of his plans."

***

Lord Crampton sat in the worn, overstuffed chair and stared at Lady Phoebe, stretched out on the bed in the posting inn they had stopped at a few hours before. She certainly was a beautiful young lady. An abundance of brown curls, highlighted with gold, were spread over the pillow. He'd removed her bonnet and took out her hairpins when he laid her down. He studied her face from her plump, deep pink lips to the lengthy lashes resting on her creamy white skin, hiding what he knew were deep blue eyes. The eyes of a siren.

The girl had spirit, too, and fought him quite hard before he was able to dose her with laudanum, which had spilled all over the coach and her person. Right now, he was admittedly a bit concerned about how long it was taking her to wake up from the drug. He didn't want to kill the chit. Hell, he didn't even want to be in her presence, couldn't wait to be done with her, and on his way back to Greece with full pockets. The only way to accomplish that was to use her. She was no more than his means to that end.

Once her mother discovered her young chick missing, and in the company of a man with no maid or other chaperone, there would be no other solution but to marry her off to him. He would get the money, bed her—since he might as well enjoy what he'd paid for with his freedom— then leave her in the country while he spent the next few years in Greece before he had to return, settle down, and fill his nursery.

It was a wonderful plan, and one he couldn't wait to see to its end.

He ran his finger around the inside of his cravat, tapped his fingertips on the arm of the chair, and wished she would wake up, so he didn't have to worry about a murder charge.

CHAPTER THIRTEEN

Selina rested her head against the back of the squab in Henry's carriage as they lumbered along to Lord Crampton's house. The only thing keeping her from crawling into her bed was the anxiety at Phoebe being in that horrible man's hands. She agreed with Henry, though. For all the terrible things about Lord Crampton, she was certain he would not physically harm Phoebe.

"You do know if this becomes public, Phoebe will be ruined?" Selina turned her head from where she watched the carriage slowly making its way through the traffic. She wanted to scream and just jump from the vehicle and race the rest of the way to her old home.

"That is the key, my love," Henry said as he took her hand in his and ran his thumb over her knuckles. "Phoebe is not out yet and is not well-known. Lord Crampton has only just returned from Greece a few weeks ago and is not as notorious as others in the *ton*. They might not be seen together by anyone who matters."

She sucked in a breath. "You don't suppose

he would physically compromise her, do you?"

"Again, I am guessing, but for all his faults, I feel underneath it all, he is a man of honor. You know Phoebe would fight him on that, and I don't think he would force her."

"Where are you getting these opinions, Henry?"

"I've learned a few things about him visiting my clubs. He is irresponsible with his estates, runs up bills with shopkeepers who he knows he can't pay, and tried to ruin you with gossip."

"Well, so far he sounds like the best of men." She smirked, not necessarily feeling the humor.

"On the other hand, it seems he had planned to raise his tenants' rent but relented when his steward pointed out the farmers would not be able to feed their families with a rent raise. He also found a young woman on the streets in Greece, bought her from her father, and she's been Crampton's mistress for several years, living quite well. Although that might not seem noble at first glance, he saved the girl from a life of misery."

"Where did he get his money before he inherited Crampton's estates?"

"He'd been the beneficiary of two very small estates in Cornwall from someone on his mother's side."

She grinned at him. "You certainly did glean a lot of information on the man. I thought it was only women who gossiped?"

"Not quite, my love. Men do just as much, only we don't let it be known, and keep it behind the walls of our clubs." He moved the curtain aside and peeked out the window. "It appears we are almost at Crampton's townhouse."

They left the carriage and climbed the stairs to the residence. A short drop of the knocker had the door opening. "Good afternoon, Stevens," Selina said.

"My lady! What a pleasure to see you. Are you to see his lordship? Because if you are, he is not at home, and I believe not expected for a couple of days."

"No, actually we are here to speak with some of the staff. May we be allowed to do that?"

He stared at her and considered the matter. It would be against procedure in all houses to allow outsiders to question the staff, but she had been their employer for years when she'd been married to Lord Crampton. "I would like to consult with Mr. Westfall."

Westfall was the head butler, and that request made perfect sense. "Yes, please do. We shall wait in the drawing room."

He bowed. "Very good. I will send in tea."

Selina was grateful for tea. For as much as she couldn't think of swallowing her tea this morning, now she found herself ravenous. Once Phoebe was back home, Selina needed to address these issues she'd been having. She most likely needed more rest. Especially if she were to be feeling her best when the girls made their come-outs. That would be a very strenuous time, and she needed her usual energy.

Perhaps she was not as young as she used to be as Henry so "lovingly" pointed out.

"Good afternoon, Lady Crampton." Westfall entered the room and bowed. "May I say you are looking splendid, and it is a pleasure to see you once again."

"Thank you, Westfall." She hesitated, wanting to get the man's cooperation but not wanting to disparage his employer, either. She decided honesty was the best approach. "It is imperative that we find out where Lord Crampton has gone. We must speak with him as quickly as possible."

If her request seemed odd, the butler did not show it. But then, good butlers—which Westfall certainly was—didn't allow their feelings to be visible. "Very good, my lady. I know you would not ask such a thing unless it was an absolute necessity. I will send in his lordship's valet, Spencer."

"Thank you."

As soon as he quit the room, Selina turned to Henry. "Odd that Crampton didn't take his valet."

Henry nodded as a footman carried a tea tray in. She eyed the offerings, and her mouth actually watered. She quickly fixed tea for her and Henry and filled her plate with three small sandwiches and two tarts. She looked up at Henry who viewed her with raised brows. "Hungry, are we?"

"I don't know why. But yes. Yet this morning, just the thought of food had my stomach roiling." She shook her head as she took a bite of a cucumber and cheese spread sandwich.

The door opened, and a man, who was obviously Crampton's valet, entered the room. He crossed the floor and stood before them.

"Please have a seat. Spencer, is it?" She smiled, trying to put the man at ease.

Henry took one look at the man and decided he had no information. He did not look at all anxious, rather more puzzled. But they put him through the normal questions while Selina ate like she'd seen her last meal days ago.

"Do you have any idea who his lordship's driver might confide in?" Henry asked as he took the lemon tart from his plate and placed it on Selina's now empty one. She grinned and nodded her thanks.

"While it is not well-known among the staff, John Coachman has had a fancy for Mollie, one of the scullery maids."

Ah, possibly a break. "Thank you, Spencer. Can you please find Mollie and ask her to join us?"

The man stood, bowed, and left the room. Henry turned to Selina. "Shall I ask for another tray to be brought in?"

Instead of treating his words as a joke—which is how he meant them to be—she studied the tray for a minute, then shook her head. "No. I think I've had enough."

While he pondered those words, Spencer returned. "My lady, my lord, Stevens tells me Mollie has gone to the market for Cook."

"Thank you," Selina said. She looked at Henry. "Now what?"

"I suggest we question some other servants until she returns."

They interviewed Cook, the housekeeper, Mrs. Dennison, then two maids and a footman before Mollie entered the room, her face flushed and a concerned countenance. She dipped a curtsy. "My lady, my lord, Cook said you wished to speak with me?"

"Yes, Mollie." Henry waved to the chair across from where they both sat on a settee. "Please have a seat."

She gingerly took a seat, her face quite pale, her fingers twisting in her lap.

"Don't be nervous, Mollie. We just want to ask you a few questions. You are not in trouble," Henry said.

The girl did not relax, which seemed normal since being questioned by two members of the nobility in her employer's house would throw any servant into a tizzy.

"I understand that you have a friendship with John Coachman?"

Her blush rose from the top of her very modest gown to her hairline. "No, my lord. I would never do anything improper."

Selina held her hand up to Henry to stop him. "His lordship does not intend to indicate anything improper is going on, believe me. We just thought he might have shared things with you that will help us locate Lord Crampton."

It was smart of Selina to not mention Phoebe or why they wanted to find Lord Crampton. Even the most loyal of servants gossiped.

"I don't know too much, my lady. John did happen to mention to me"—she cast Selina a glance under lowered eyelids—"that he was taking his lordship to the shops and then he would be needed to drive him to an inn not far outside of town. He didn't expect to return today, I don't believe."

At last they had information they could use. "You would not by any chance know which inn he was stopping at, do you?"

She shook her head. "No, my lord. He never said."

Henry smiled at the young girl. "Thank you so much, Mollie. You have been a help."

"May I go?" She looked more than anxious to leave their presence.

"Yes. You may return to your duties. And thank you again."

The girl rose and scurried from the room. Henry turned to Selina. "At least we have a lead."

"But, Henry, there are dozens of inns outside of London. We don't even know in which direction they went." The fatigue on her face was beginning to concern him.

He tapped his chin with his finger. "I have an idea." He left the room and sought out the butler again. "Can you please summon Lord Crampton's valet once again?"

"Yes. Of course." The man made his way up the stairs as Henry returned to the drawing room.

Selina sat on the settee, her head resting on the back of the sofa, her hands loose in her lap, her eyes closed, and based on her heavy breathing, fast asleep. He allowed her the rest, and right before the door opened to admit Spencer, a thought raced through his mind that had his brows flying toward his hairline and his stomach twisting in knots.

"You wished to see me again, my lord?"

His head whipped toward the door as his heart thudded. "Yes." He nudged Selina, who opened her eyes and looked around. "Spencer, please have a seat." His voice cracked, but he couldn't lose control now. Not until he spoke with Spencer and then had Selina alone.

"Do you happen to know what inn your employer prefers when he travels outside of London?"

The man didn't take long to answer the question. "Yes. As a matter of fact, I do. We always stay at the White Horse Inn. It is not too far outside of London, but Lord Crampton seems to always be unable to leave early enough to put many hours in the first day when we travel, so we usually end up there."

Henry hopped up and grabbed Selina's hand. "Thank you, Spencer. You have been a great help."

He dragged her out of the room, grabbed their belongings at the door from Stevens, and hurried down to his carriage.

"Henry, for heaven's sake, you are dragging me along."

Sweat dripped down his back as he helped Selina into the carriage, gave instructions to the driver, settled across from her, and slammed the door.

"Whatever is the matter with you, Henry?" She straightened her skirts and glared at him.

He rubbed his eyes with the heels of his hands. Then he moved across the space and sat alongside her, taking her hand in his. "Selina, I must ask you a very personal question."

"You are behaving quite strangely, Henry."

"Indeed. I am feeling quite strange, truth be known."

She shook her head and covered her mouth with her hand to stifle a yawn. "What is your question?"

He swallowed a few times, then cupped her cheeks and looked her in the eye. "When was the last time you had your courses?"

CHAPTER FOURTEEN

Selina stared at him. In a matter of moments her expression went from puzzled, to thoughtful, to surprised, to happy, to tears. "Oh, my goodness. I am ruined! My girls are ruined! I've ruined their lives. They will never make a successful match. They will die unhappy spinsters unless I bury myself in the country and let Lady Penrose see to their come-out. If she will, that is. She probably won't because I'm ruined."

She threw herself into his arms and sobbed. Then she pulled away and glared at him. "This is all your fault."

"My apologies, madam, but how is this all my fault? The last time I gave this any consideration at all, it took two people to create a child."

"A child, Henry!" She beat his chest. "How can I be having a child? I am too old."

"Indeed? How old are you, Selina?"

"Five and thirty. Even you said," she glowered at him, "that I am no longer young." She took the handkerchief he handed her and blew her nose. She might be five and thirty, but at the moment she looked more like her daughters' age.

She dropped her head into her hands. "What shall I do? This is terrible."

"Pardon me, my dear, but I think the creation of a child is a wonderful thing."

Raising her head, she scowled. "Not under these circumstances."

He took her chin between his thumb and index finger. "Under any circumstances, a babe is a precious thing."

"Oh, Henry, you are such a wonderful father." She dropped her head into her hands again. "What will I do?"

Henry looked out the window. They had almost reached the end of town. It would be less than an hour before they reached their destination. "There is no 'you,' Selina. We are in this together, and we will solve the issue together. Now, you will calm yourself and be prepared to confront Crampton and get Phoebe back. Right now our biggest concern is making sure *she* is not ruined."

"How can you say that? If what we suspect is true, I will give birth to a bastard."

"No!" He took her ice-cold hands in his. "This child could very well be a boy, and therefore, my only heir. He will *not* be born a bastard."

She flung herself into his arms again. He remembered from when his deceased wife carried his girls how unpredictable her behavior had been. Apparently, all women behaved in this mystifying manner when increasing.

He gathered her into his arms and rested her head on his chest. Within minutes, she was sound asleep. He smiled. Could not help it. This was a mess, true, but a child! At his age. Well, he wasn't all that old, merely six and forty.

A bastard.

No child of his would be born with that moniker. He had no idea how this would be resolved, but Selina would not bear his child while unwed.

The carriage slowed and rocked as it rode over holes in the ground when they approached the White Horse Inn. Henry had not been to this inn before, but from the looks of how poorly the grounds were kept, it didn't appear he had missed anything.

He tapped Selina on her cheek. "Wake up, sweetheart. We're at the inn."

She smiled at him, her face flushed from sleep, and his heart turned over. He had no idea where they would go from here, but he loved her and would protect her from scandal. As well as their child.

***

Lord Crampton breathed a sigh of relief when Phoebe opened her eyes. Her lashes fluttered and she looked around the room with confusion.

"Where am I?" She sat up, then pressed her hand to her head. "Goodness, I'm dizzy."

"Perhaps you should lie back down again."

She did as he suggested but scowled at him. "Whatever were you thinking? Do you presume kidnapping me will benefit you in some way?"

He crossed his arms over his chest. "Yes, I do. Once we are discovered together, you will be ruined and forced to marry me. I will then have control of your money."

She eased herself back up, leaning on the headboard. "What money? I have none, and you received it all when Papa died."

He snorted. "I received the entailed properties but no money."

She looked genuinely surprised. "Where did it all go?"

"To you. And your sister."

"That is not possible." She shrugged. "Mama had to work as a chaperone to support us after Papa died. If you have no money, then there is no money."

"If you think you are so sure of yourself, perhaps you might look into it further. That is why you must marry me."

"I have no intention of marrying you."

"You will once word gets out. And I will make sure it does."

Phoebe waved her hand. "You are delusional. No matter how horrible this looks, I will not marry you."

Crampton leaned forward. Why in heaven's name hadn't he kidnapped the more timid sister? But then he knew why. This scheme of his would lead to marriage, and he felt a more spirited girl would be a better idea for when he had to leave Greece and return to start his nursery. "You mother will not allow you to face a scandal."

"My mother will not allow me to marry *you*." She swung her legs over the edge of the bed and stood, holding onto the bed post. "You must leave now."

His jaw dropped. "What? Do you not understand I have kidnapped you and you are my prisoner?"

"Hah. Prisoner, indeed." She took a few steps toward him. "I have need of the chamber pot. Please leave and allow me some privacy."

Crampton looked around the space. The room was on the second floor, and he doubted the girl had enough of her wits about her to climb out successfully. "Very well. But I will be right outside the door. If you take too long, privacy or no privacy, I will return."

She waved him off as if he were no more than a bothersome insect. He apparently had not put any fear into the girl. She acted as though she were the one in charge.

He stepped outside and leaned against the wall, considering where to go from here. He knew, without a doubt, that Pomeroy would find him, but he had hoped to force Phoebe downstairs to eat dinner before that, making sure they were seen. He hadn't expected her to take so long to wake up.

It had been bad enough trying to convince the innkeeper that he needed to carry the chit into the inn and up the stairs because she had fainted. Now, he was obviously going to have a problem getting her downstairs. Young girls were supposed to be frightened easily, whimpering, crying. This one was more annoyed than anything else.

He turned and knocked on the door. "I am coming in. You've had long enough."

When she didn't respond, he cracked the door open and looked it. She straddled the window sill, looking down. He raced across the room and grabbed her arm. Bloody hell, he didn't want the girl to kill herself.

"Let go of me." She tugged her arm and almost fell. He grabbed her around the waist and pulled her back into the room. "Are you addlepated? That fall will kill you."

She wrestled away from him and faced him with her hands on her hips. "No. I will probably do no more damage than a broken leg."

They both swung around as the door to the room crashed open. Pomeroy and Lady Crampton stood in the doorway.

Bloody, bloody hell.

"Phoebe, are you all right?" Selina hurried across the room and yanked her daughter away from Crampton and glared at him. "Did he touch you?"

"Of course, I didn't touch her. I only wanted to ruin her so she would be forced to marry me."

Henry strode up to the man, pulled his arm back, and plowed into his face. The sound of bone breaking had Phoebe and Selina cringing.

Crampton landed on the floor, holding his nose, staring up at Henry. "I didn't hurt her. Bloody hell, I didn't even frighten her. She's a spirited little chit."

Henry reached down, pulled Crampton up by his cravat, and threw a punch into his middle. "Do. Not. Speak of her that way."

Crampton leaned over, holding his middle. "Now she must marry me."

Selina drew herself up. "She will certainly not marry you, you dreadful man."

Henry pushed the man's shoulder, so he landed on the bed, still holding his middle.

"What if word gets out that she was here with me? Alone." Crampton scrambled back when Henry raised his fist again. "No, never mind. Bad plan. No harm was done. No one saw us, and my driver would not say anything."

"If I hear anything about this incident I will come for you, and you better be prepared to meet me with your second at dawn." Henry took Phoebe and Selina by the arm. "Let us depart. We can make it home tonight."

He hurried them down the stairs and to the side door next to the bottom step, avoiding the common room. He stopped just before they exited. "I'll be right back."

He approached the innkeeper and gestured to where Selina and Phoebe stood. "This young lady was not here tonight, and there is a gentleman upstairs in need of medical assistance." He reached into his pocket, withdrew some coins, and dropped them on the bar in front of the innkeeper.

The man nodded, and Henry returned to them. "Our carriage awaits."

***

The next afternoon Henry dropped the knocker on Lady Penrose's front door after receiving a note from Selina. Once he was led into the drawing room, he found Selina, Phoebe, Prudence, Elise, Juliet, and Marigold, all seated like quite the ladies, their hands folded demurely in their laps, studying him as if he were an insect under glass. To say he was taken aback was an understatement. "What goes on here?"

Phoebe stood and waved him to a chair. "Please take a seat." Then she walked to Selina and extended her hand. When her mother took it, Phoebe led her to where Henry sat. "Sit." At Selina's raised brows, she added, "Please."

Why did he feel as though he—or they—

were in a bit of trouble?

Phoebe clasped her hands behind her back and paced. "Prudence and I made a visit today to Mr. Darwin."

"The solicitor?" Selina asked.

Phoebe nodded. "The very one."

Prudence jumped up and joined her sister, wrapping her arm around her waist, as they stood in front of them. "We don't want the money."

"What are you talking about?" Selina was quite pale, her words barely above a whisper.

Prudence sat next to Selina. "It took some persuasion," she grinned, "but Mr. Darwin told us the contents of Papa's will. How you got nothing, Lord Crampton got the properties but no money, and Phoebe and I get all the money for our dowries, our Season and whatever is left over."

"That would be correct." Selina glanced at Henry, who felt as perplexed as she looked.

"But." Phoebe sat next to Henry, making the four of them quite crowded on the settee as they all shifted over. Juliet, Marigold, and Elise watched from across the room, smirks on their lovely faces. Where the devil were their husbands? Most likely off enjoying cards and brandy, while he was cosseted with females. He tugged on his cravat, a bit uncomfortable with all these women staring at him.

"The only way we get the money is if Mama doesn't re-marry."

"This does not concern you, girls," Selina said. "Your Papa wanted you to have his money."

Phoebe snorted. "Hardly. Papa didn't want us to have his money, he wanted to control everyone from the grave."

Selina looked at Henry and shrugged.

"Anyway, Mama. He might have given us life, but Lord Pomeroy has given us love." Phoebe covered Henry's hand with hers. "We feel as though you are our true papa. We've lived with you for four years and have grown to love you."

Prudence reached across Selina and took Henry's other hand. "Yes, you are our true papa." With all these females, two of them holding his hands, one sitting so close he wanted nothing more than to lead her upstairs to the bedroom, and three others staring at him from across the room, he felt as though all the air had left the room. He stood and tugged on his waistcoat. "If you will excuse me for a moment."

With all eyes on him, he strode across the room and poured himself a very large glass of brandy. He took a deep swallow, swirled the liquid around, and took another swallow. He closed his eyes as the brandy slid down his throat, warming his chest and stomach. "Are we finished?"

"No!" Five female voices joined together with outrage. He glanced over at Selina who looked like she wanted to escape herself. Maybe they could make a run for it. Cross the room, grab her hand, and head for the front entrance. Then he remembered her condition and considered that racing around the house might upset her stomach and cause her last meal to make a reappearance in a most unpleasant manner.

Elise stood. "Papa, please sit down. What Prudence and Phoebe want to say to you is very important."

He reluctantly returned to the nest of female hens and took his seat.

"We know you love Mama, and she loves you. We also know the reason she refuses to marry you is because of that foolish will." Phoebe took his hand once more. He put the other hand in his pocket to avoid another cross-body hand-holding session.

"We all decided," Prudence's arm swept the room, encompassing his daughters as well as her sister, "that your happiness is more important than money."

Juliet leaned forward. "Elise, Marigold, and I have agreed to sponsor the girls next Season so you don't have to worry about the cost."

"The cost!" Henry hopped up.

He turned in a circle to encompass all the women. "This nonsense has gone far enough. Yes, I love your mother, and she loves me. For reasons of which you are unaware, it has now come to our attention that it is quite necessary for us to marry." He stopped when all five girls gasped and laid their hands on their chests in unison. Attempting to prevent the female hysteria about to erupt, he continued, directing his comments to Prudence and Phoebe. "I am honored by your suggestion, however, I strongly advise you not to throw away everything you have coming to you."

Phoebe jumped up. Or was it Prudence? When the girls were together he oftentimes had a problem telling them apart. "No. We refuse the money. We have already told Mr. Darwin we refuse the money." She placed her hand over her heart and closed her eyes. "It is for the greater good." Whichever girl this one was, she could make quite a career on Drury Lane had she not been the daughter of a viscount.

Henry ran his fingers through his hair. "If you are sure you wish to relinquish the money, I will gladly pay your dowries and for your Seasons."

He looked over at Juliet and glared. "I can certainly afford it."

The stunned silence was broken by Selina's words. "Can we send for tea? I am quite famished."

CHAPTER FIFTEEN

As they waited for the tea to arrive, all the women gathered together and not one voice rose above another, yet they all seemed to be able to follow several conversations at once. The chatter from six women was enough to drive a man to drink.

A most pleasant idea.

Pomeroy refilled his glass and took a sip, studying all these women who had invaded his life. He nearly choked on his next swallow when he remembered this all had started because he wanted to be free of his three daughters' clothing bills and had come up with the "marry in order of your birth" scheme to get Elise, lovely stubborn woman that she was, thinking about marriage, which she had eschewed most of her life.

By marrying Selina and taking on the expense of her two daughters, he was virtually back where he started from. Three women. Mountains of bills. Ah, at least he could afford it.

He cleared his throat to gain the women's attention to no avail. He tried again. The noise only grew louder. He really needed to get some peace and quiet and was certain he could track down his sons-in-law and other male companions at his club.

"Ladies."

They ignored him.

"Ladies, may I speak?"

They ignored him.

"Ladies!"

Even his raised voiced gained him nothing. If anything, the sound grew, possibly to drown him out.

Desperate, he placed his thumb and index finger in his mouth and whistled.

Six heads swiveled in his direction. "Yes, dear?" Selina asked.

"I see you are all enjoying your visit. I will be leaving you now so you won't be bothered by my presence."

"I didn't realize you were still here," Marigold said.

"Well, then, I wish you all a good evening." He gave a formal bow.

"Wait!" Elise stood. "We must arrange for the proposal."

"What?"

"The proposal," Juliet said. "You know it is a family tradition that all proposals are made in front of everyone."

His heart thumped and sweat broke out all over his body. In his life, Henry had faced an enemy on the battlefield, a wife in labor three times, and his man of business each month as he presented him with his daughters' bills. Nothing, however, terrified him more than the thought of getting down on bended knee in front of the entire family and proposing to Selina.

He cleared his throat. "Er, that won't be necessary. You see, I have already asked Lady Crampton to marry me numerous times."

"But she always said no," Phoebe added.

"So you must ask again, properly, and in front of us all."

Did he see a smirk of satisfaction on Elise's face? After all, she was the first one subjected to this "all of the family be present for the proposal" tradition.

He really had to escape. There was no air in the room, and the women all started up again. Speaking above each other, waving their hands in the air. "Ladies!"

Again he was ignored.

All right, he had tried. It was time to abscond. He edged his way out of the room, quietly closing the door, and strode down the corridor. He grabbed his hat and cane from the butler and made his exit.

The fresh air and numbing silence made him grin and do a little tap dance.

***

Selina patted her face with a clean, wet cloth. She had just brought up the tea and toast she'd forced herself to eat that morning. She had passed completely on luncheon, but now she would have to sit with Henry, his daughters, their husbands, and Phoebe and Prudence to eat dinner and have Henry do his formal proposal. If things remained the same tonight as they had been the last week, her stomach would settle down before they ate.

Truth be known, she thought the family's tradition of "in front of the whole family" proposal was quite sweet. She knew Henry was terrified, but she would rather enjoy being accepted into his family this way.

"Mama, are you ready?" Phoebe tapped on her door.

"Yes, dear." She picked up her gloves, reticule, and shawl and crossed the room. Her daughters stood there looking absolutely beautiful. They would certainly have a successful Season.

They both kissed her on the cheek, and the three of them descended the stairs of Lady Penrose's townhouse and climbed into the carriage Henry had sent for them. Their hostess had retired to her sister's estate in Bedfordshire, leaving Selina and the girls with instructions to have the house closed for the winter after she and Henry married and they all moved into his townhouse.

Despite the proposal taking place tonight, the wedding had already been planned for the following Friday. Henry saw no reason to wait, and with her increasing, she had to agree. She shook her head at these thoughts, still stunned at being with child at her age. Not that she was so very old, but with grown daughters, it was the last thing she'd ever thought would happen to her. She smiled and laid her hand on her belly as the carriage rolled away.

The sound of cheerful chatter greeted her and the girls as they entered Henry's library. His daughters and their husbands had already arrived and were enjoying pre-dinner drinks and lively conversation.

"Ah, here they are now." Henry broke away from the group and headed toward her, kissing her on the cheek and bowing to the girls.

They joined the others and after only a few minutes of conversation, the butler announced dinner. No formal line-up, they strolled into the dining room chatting away and settled into their places, with Henry at the head and her seated to his right. The footman began laying platters and bowls on the table and pouring wine.

Now that her stomach felt better, she found she was quite hungry. The food was delicious, no surprise there since during the four years she'd lived in Henry's house, she'd always admired the Cook's offerings.

Since Selina was not yet the official hostess of Pomeroy's house, she left it up to Elise to announce tea in the drawing room for the ladies. When it appeared they were all looking toward her, she raised her chin. "Ladies, if you will join me in the drawing room, we will give the gentlemen time to enjoy their after-dinner drinks.

***

"Lady Crampton, have you decided on a gown for your wedding?" Juliet viewed her over the rim of her teacup.

"I have a lovely pale blue gown that I've only worn a few times that I think will do nicely."

"Mama, you are always cautious when it comes to money," Phoebe said. "You should have a new gown made up."

"Nonsense. My blue gown will do just fine." She was quite aware of the fact that Henry was taking on expenses for not just her, but for Phoebe and Prudence, as well. Their Seasons and dowries would cost the poor man quite a bit. The least she could do was hold down her purchases.

"I agree with Phoebe," Henry said as he and the other men joined the women. "You shall have a new gown for your wedding."

"No, Henry. I will not. My blue gown is perfect."

"Papa, I believe you are stalling." Marigold smirked in his direction.

Goodness, Henry did look a bit peaked. Like she felt in the mornings, pale and as if his last meal was coming back up.

"Yes, Henry, you made us all do it," Lord Hertford said. He grinned at his wife, Juliet.

"And now it is your turn, Pomeroy," the Viscount St. George chimed in, as he sat alongside his wife, Elise, taking her hand in his.

"Very well." Henry crossed the room to her. "I just want you all to know this was unnecessary since I've already proposed to Lady Crampton."

"On your knees." Lord Stanley grinned at his wife, Marigold. He'd been the last man to do the public proposal. Selina remembered it well, along with Juliet's proposal. Elise's had happened before she'd met Henry.

She had to admit her heart took a few extra beats when Henry dropped to one knee and took her hand in his. He looked so handsome

And terrified. She loved him so much.

"My dear Lady Crampton. Will you make me the happiest man in all the kingdom and become my wife?"

Selina burst into tears.

***

It was three weeks past the wedding. Phoebe and Prudence were in the music room practicing their dance steps while Selina sat on the settee in Henry's study and worked on some sort of thing she assured him was a blanket for their babe. He'd tried several times to hide the awful thing, afraid if she actually finished it and instructed the nurse to wrap the child in it, the poor mite would probably strangle with all the loose ends. Somehow he didn't think blankets were supposed to look like that.

That morning when he'd made love to his wife he noticed her bump was growing. Her initial sickness early in the day had passed, and with the way she was eating she would probably give birth to a child big enough to come out of her womb demanding a roast beef dinner.

"My lord, Lord Crampton has called." The butler held out Crampton's card.

Henry looked over at Selina, both of them with raised eyebrows.

"Very well, show the man in."

Crampton entered the room and bowed to them. "Good afternoon, my lord, my lady."

"Crampton." Henry gave him a brief nod. "Please have a seat."

They hadn't seen the man since they'd left him bleeding in the inn where he'd taken Phoebe. Selina had sent along a note to Mr. Darwin, advising him of her marriage. He'd sent back a warm congratulatory note and advised her that due to the terms of her late husband's will, her daughters would no longer have the use of the funds set aside for their Season and dowries.

No surprise there so Selina simply returned a note thanking him for his congratulations.

"What can I do for you, Crampton?" Henry sat back in the comfortable chair behind his desk and studied the man with not exactly an icy regard, but certainly not a warm one.

"I have come to apologize to both of you."

They waited to hear what else Crampton had to say. He hopped up and began to pace. "I never, ever should have taken your daughter, Lady Pomeroy. That was not well done of me." He stopped in front of her. "I was desperate for the money, but I have since realized my lack of funds was my fault, and my fault alone."

When neither Henry nor Selina responded, he continued. "I am eternally grateful that the girl was not ruined because of my actions."

Henry shifted in his chair. "Whether your apology is accepted or not depends on my wife. Your actions caused her a great deal of distress."

"Yes, I know, and I am extremely sorry for that." He looked at Selina. "Whether you forgive me or not, I want you to know that I will place sufficient funds into an account for your daughters' Season expenses and dowries."

Henry shook his head. "No need for that, Crampton. I can well afford to take care of the girls."

"No, I insist."

"No, *I* insist."

Selina held up her hand. "Just a moment, please." She turned in his direction. "Henry, I think you are being foolish."

"No, my dear. I'm not. The girls are my responsibility now."

"Then what if we allow Lord Crampton to supply the dowries, and you take care of the expenses."

Henry stared at her for a minute. "Very well, but I will add to their dowries.

Crampton looked relieved and bowed once more. "I will not keep you from your duties." He took Selina's hand and held it for a moment. "Congratulations on your marriage. I wish you happy." He glanced at the knitted mess in her lap. "I am sure your … will be lovely when it is finished." He offered her a warm smile.

"It's a blanket."

"Yes, of course it is. Very nice." He moved toward the door. "Well, good afternoon, then."

Crampton was gone for a few minutes when Selina held up her knitting. "Do you think this looks like a blanket, Henry?"

"Most definitely, my dear."

They were interrupted when the butler carried in the tea tray.

"Thank you, Mason, just place it over there on the table." She stood and shook out her skirts. "Tea has arrived, Henry."

He pushed his ledger aside and joined her. She poured tea, fixed it how he liked it, and handed it to him, along with a plate of small tarts and the horrible ladies' sandwiches. He sighed.

At least for a while he'd had decent tea food. He glanced over at Selina who took a sip of her tea and smiled at him. Yes, he'd rather have his wife than hearty sandwiches.

But once in a while….

EPILOGUE

March, 1823
London, England

Henry paced the floor in his library, his heart thumping each time another woman ran up or down the stairs. He checked his timepiece again. Had it taken this long for his daughters to be born?

"Pomeroy, let me pour you another glass of brandy. Believe me, when Elise was giving birth that helped a great deal." St. George called to him from where he sat with his four-year-old daughter, Allison, on his lap.

The little girl looked up from the story book she'd been looking at, all big blue eyes and golden curls. "Grandpapa, you can read my book with me."

Warmth spread from his middle to his face. He loved that little girl, just as he loved all his grandchildren. All girls. Elise had two, Allison and Mary Grace. Juliet and Marigold each had one, Penelope and Kathleen. He sighed. Three daughters, two step-daughters, four granddaughters.

"I would love that, Poppet." He plucked her from her daddy's lap and settled her in his lap. This was just what he needed, a way to distract him from what was going on upstairs. He had tried to enter the room a little while ago and was immediately told in no uncertain terms to return to the library.

Phoebe and Prudence had not wanted to attend the afternoon tea they had received an invitation to, but Selina had sent word from the bedchamber that Lady Truedale was going to chaperone them and they should not bypass the tea. As young, unmarried ladies they were forbidden from being present at their mother's bedside during childbirth.

The Season had not officially started, but slowly members of the *ton* were arriving in London and events were beginning to spring up. Selina had arranged for a chaperone for the girls for the first few weeks until she would be able to attend herself.

Four books and two brandies later, Elise stood at the doorway, her face aglow. "Papa, you must come upstairs."

"The babe is here?"

"Yes."

"And Selina?"

"Is fine." He breathed a sigh of relief and turned to the three men who had started a card game. "I'm a papa again!"

They all cheered, and then returned to their game. He had to remember they had all gone through it recently, so he allowed their lack of enthusiasm.

"Come." Elise held out her hand.

He tried to maintain his dignity as he headed to the stairs but found himself bounding up, two steps at a time to get to his wife. He burst into the bedchamber. Marigold and Juliet stood next to Selina, their smiles bright, their faces beaming.

Selina held her hand out. She looked tired, very tired. "Come meet your new baby."

Eschewing dignity, he climbed onto the bed alongside her. She held a little bundle in her arms. A small mewing sound came from within the soft blanket.

"What shall we name her?" he asked as he touched the tip of his finger to her soft skin.

"I don't know. I was thinking about Michael. What say you?"

He continued to stare at the baby touching her soft hair. "That's a rather odd name for a girl."

"But not so strange for a boy."

His head jerked up to look at her. "Did you say a boy?"

Selina laughed. "Yes, my lord. You have a son."

He unfolded the blanket, tugged down the nappy, and looked. "It's a boy!"

His three daughters, along with his wife, burst into laughter. "Yes, Papa, we have a brother," Marigold said.

A knock on the door drew him from admiring his son. St. George, Hertford, and Stanley crowded into the room. "Pomeroy, rumor has it you have a boy." St. George shifted Allison from one arm to the other.

"Yes, I do." He still had a hard time believing it. "I even checked."

"This requires a celebration," Stanley said. "I say we all retire to the drawing room and open a bottle of champagne."

"If you will excuse me, gentlemen, I prefer to take a nap." Selina handed the babe to the newly employed nurse.

"Yes, of course, my dear. We will celebrate now, and then again, when you are able to join us."

After giving her a thorough kiss and thanking her for giving him a son, he trooped downstairs and joined the rest of his family.

He looked around as they all chatted with each other, while Mason went around the room and poured the champagne. Henry held up his glass. "To Michael, the Viscount Munthorpe."

"Who is that?" Allison said as she stared up at Henry.

He squatted down and looked her in the eye. "He is your…" He turned to Elise. "What is Michael to Allison?"

"Let me see. He would be Allison's uncle."

"But he's a baby!" she said. "And, he's a boy." She wrinkled her nose. "I don't like boys."

"Ah, but you will one day, Poppet."

"No, I won't, Grandpapa. Mama's friend brought her son to visit with us and he refused to have tea with me and my dollies."

Henry tapped her on her adorable little nose. "You should have served brandy."

"Papa!" his three daughters said at once.

Ah, daughters!

The End

Did you like this story? Please consider leaving a review on either Goodreads or the place where you bought it. Long or short, your review will help other readers discover new authors and make purchasing decisions!

I hope you had fun reading Selina and Henry's love story. If you want more Regency romance, you might enjoy reading *Seducing the Marquess,* book 1 in the Lords & Ladies in Love series.

London, 1819. Richard, Marquess of Devon is satisfied with his ton marriage. His wife of five months, Lady Eugenia Devon, thought she was, too, until she found the book. Their marriage is one of respect and affection, with no messy entanglements such as love. Devon's upbringing impressed upon him that gentlemen slake their baser needs on a mistress, not their gently bred wives. However, once married, he was no longer comfortable bedding a woman other Eugenia. When she stumbles onto a naughty book, she begins a campaign to change the rules.

Lady Eugenia wants her very proper husband to fall in love with her. But her much changed and undeniably wicked behavior might inadvertently drive her confused husband to ponder the unthinkable—his perfect Lady has taken a lover. But the only man Eugenia only wants is her husband. The book can bring sizzling desire to the marriage or it might cause an explosion.

If you've already read *Seducing the Marquess*, you can find a list of all my books on my website: http://calliehutton.com/

For the special treat I promised you,
Go to
https://www.subscribepage.com/f3b6d8_copy
to receive a free copy of
A Little Bit of Romance, three short stories of lovers reunited.
Enjoy!

ABOUT THE AUTHOR

Callie Hutton, the *USA Today* bestselling author of *The Elusive Wife,* writes both Western Historical and Regency romance, with "historic elements and sensory details" (*The Romance Reviews*). She also pens an occasional contemporary or two. Callie lives in Oklahoma with several rescue dogs and her top cheerleader husband of many years. Her family also includes her daughter, son, daughter-in-law and twin grandsons affectionately known as "The Twinadoes."

Callie loves to hear from readers. Contact her directly at calliehutton11@gmail.com or find her online at www.calliehutton.com. Sign up for her newsletter to receive information on new releases, appearances, contests and exclusive subscriber content. Visit her on Facebook, Twitter and Goodreads.

Callie Hutton has written more than thirty books. For a complete listing, go to www.calliehutton.com/books

Praise for books by Callie Hutton

A Wife by Christmas

"A *Wife by Christmas* is the reason why we read

romance...the perfect story for any season." --The Romance Reviews Top Pick

The Elusive Wife

"I loved this book and you will too. Jason is a hottie & Oliva is the kind of woman we'd all want as a friend. Read it!" --Cocktails and Books

"In my experience I've had a few hits but more misses with historical romance so I was really pleasantly surprised to be hooked from the start by obviously good writing." --Book Chick City

"The historic elements and sensory details of each scene make the story come to life, and certainly helps immerse the reader in the world that Olivia and Jason share." --The Romance Reviews

"You will not want to miss *The Elusive Wife*." --My Book Addiction

"...it was a well written plot and the characters were likeable." --Night Owl Reviews

A Run for Love

"An exciting, heart-warming Western love story!" --*NY Times* bestselling author Georgina Gentry

"I loved this book!!! I read the BEST historical romance last night...It's called *A Run For Love.*" -- *NY Times* bestselling author Sharon Sala

"This is my first Callie Hutton story, but it certainly won't be my last." --The Romance Reviews

A Prescription for Love

"There was love, romance, angst, some darkness, laughter, hope and despair." --RomCon

"I laughed out loud at some of the dialogue and situations. I think you will enjoy this story by Callie Hutton." --Night Owl Reviews

An Angel in the Mail

"...a warm fuzzy sensuous read. I didn't put it down until I was done." --Sizzling Hot Reviews

Visit www.calliehutton.com for more information.

8048

90856727R00102

Made in the USA
Middletown, DE
26 September 2018